THE RAT-TAKER

THE RAT-TAKER

a novel by
Shirleyann Costigan

QP Books
New Orleans, Louisiana

Published in 2014 by QP Books, an imprint of Quid Pro Books. Also available in leading ebook formats.

ISBN 978-1-61027-278-0 (pbk)

QUID PRO BOOKS
Quid Pro, LLC
5860 Citrus Blvd., Suite D-101
New Orleans, Louisiana 70123
www.qpbooks.com

This is a work of fiction. The characters, names, events, dialogue, and circumstances are imaginary or are used fictionally. Any resemblance to real persons or actual events is purely coincidental, fictitious, or imaginary.

Cover: *"La vendeur de mort-aux-rats"* by Rembrandt Harmenszoon van Rijn.

"Brown rat (Mus decumanus)" vintage illustration from Meyers Konversations-Lexik, 1897, copyright © Hein Nouwens, courtesy of ShutterStock, Inc.

Book design by Katherine Fatica.

Publisher's Cataloging-in-Publication

Costigan, Shirleyann.
   The rat-taker : [a novel of the middle ages] / Shirleyann Costigan.
        p. cm.
   1. England—History—14th century—Fiction. 2. Middle Ages—Fiction. I. Title.
   II. Costigan, Shirleyann.

PS3619.A56423 C18 2014

ABOUT THE AUTHOR

Shirleyann Costigan, an educator, writer, and editor, received her M.A. in English Studies from Loyola University, Los Angeles. Before beginning her long career as a writer for school publishing, she was an elementary school teacher in Pacoima, California, then an Instructor of English at Mount St. Mary College, New Hampshire. She has since worked both freelance and in-house for numerous school publishers including Boston Educational Research in Boston, Massachusetts, and five years as Writing Director for Hampton-Brown Publishing in Carmel, California. She is currently a part-time editor/writer for National Geographic School Publishing in Washington D.C. Shirleyann now lives in Baja, California, Mexico with her two schnauzers and many happy memories. *The Rat-Taker* is her first novel.

ACKNOWLEDGMENTS

My deepest appreciation goes to George Murphy, a most resourceful man whose energy and enthusiasm is exceeded only by his generosity. Many thanks, George. Without you, *The Rat-Taker* would still be an unfulfilled dream.

DEDICATION

To my Mom and Dad

THE RAT-TAKER

From the Journal of Jonathan Purchell
19 March, Anno Domini 1375

My name is Jonathan Purchell, Clarke and Scrivener for Master Simon Ratiker; beyond that, there is nothing you need know of me. Let me say only that a series of unhappy circumstances have placed me in the employ of a man I despise.

Why I despise Simon Ratiker is as yet unclear to me, and I admit this with some confusion. He employs my pen to maintain his legers and record his remembrances. Now I will use my pen as an instrument to explore my own feelings about him. I will begin with a description of the man, for I believe that outward signs do bespeak of a person's inner spirit. So, too, may a man's words and actions reflect, however obliquely, a secret self never openly revealed. Yet why unrevealed, for reasons good or reasons ill, it is hard for us to know.

Simon Ratiker is a man such. He stands tall and stiff backed, though he moves with a rare grace for his age, which I reckon to be about fifty-five. His hair is yellow as straw, thin, and waxy. He keeps it under a felt cap, which I have never seen him without. I think he wears it to bed. His bones are good, but the flesh of his face sags and is sallow. Not a handsome man by any account, and I would forbear to dwell on his looks if it were not for his eyes.

It is his eyes that warrant attention, for aside from a false twinkle set in place when he wishes to deceive or cajole, his eyes are like dead men's graves: black pits swallowing all they see with dispassionate greed, giving back nothing. They are without soul, his eyes. Aye, it is as hard as that. Simon Ratiker has no soul, upon my own I do swear. In due course I believe I shall have evidence for this judgment. Then shall I set the man down piece-by-piece, display all his parts, so I may discover for myself that which is missing.

Veritate en scribo,
Johannes P.

I remember the day the rats began to die. History does not mark that day, yet my own history is contained wholly within it and of my history I am the truest witness. So central is that day to my life I return to it again and again. Yet never do I reach the end. Nor will I, it seems, until all my days are ended.

Simon Ratiker
London, Anno Domini 1375

Simon begins dictating his narrative

T hat day in 1348, the day that became the cross point of my life where all that came before and all that follows after does meet and entwine, began with Maude. I awoke to her embrace, to her flesh exciting my flesh, to her hunger that readily fed my own, her unholy appetites exciting the illusion that she loved me.

Why do I say *illusion*? My very name will tell you why. I am Simon the Rat Taker or, as I came to be known, Simon Ratiker. I am not a man to be loved, not a man to be admired, nor even remembered.

Nor am I a man of letters. My attempts to write my own thoughts are pitiful in the extreme; thus do I depend on my scrivener, Jonathan Purchell, to make my meaning clear. He is most skilled, this Jonathan, a man who listens then polishes and sets each word into its proper place as if it were a work of silver. When he reads back what I have said, I marvel at how my thoughts, naturally careless and unfixed, roll out orderly, precise, made permanent on the page. Hearing them thus, I grow hungry for more memories and greedy for words.

I was born in Cornwall. Why I abandoned my village is a story I will tell anon. For now I say only that I, like my father, my father's father, and his father, too, worked in the tin mines of Porthtowan. But before that, I played as free as any child on the windy moor that surrounded my village. Years later, those days of my earliest youth became the dreams of my nights. By day, as I scoured the dark corners of London in search of vermin, my waking dream was to return to Cornwall, not to the pit but to the clean air and broad horizons of the sea and the moor.

That was never to be. As we lay abed that autumn morning, Maude biting me with her pointy teeth, the plague had already invaded the southern coast of England. The London wardens had closed the gates against the pestilence, had raised barricades and enforced quarantines meant to keep contagion out, but news of the plague's relentless progress continued to seep into the city, infecting its citizens with fear. We all knew a reckoning was coming, driving sinners to seek repentance or, as with me, the comfort of a lover's arms.

Maude had slipped into my bed just as the bells of St. Michael Paternoster broke apart my dream. She was my master's concubine, his alone or, God help her, she would feel the blow of his fist; but that only made our forbidden love-pleasures sweeter. She was fearless, my Maude, and for that more exciting to me. The fact that she belonged to my master and could never be entirely mine was no deterrent to my desire.

We made love in silence, a necessary restraint that only intensified our pleasure. But on this day, Maude's need surpassed all restraint. She screamed at the moment of our release, and just as suddenly needles of pain pierced my head. Then came a sharper blow that for a moment did take my senses. I may have even swooned, for the next I knew Maude was champing my shoulder. "Pay attention!" she scolded. For a moment more I lay inert, stunned. The pain had passed, but I was afraid to move lest the agony return. "Hush, Maude," I whispered. "You have roused the master for certes."

"He's sick with last night's drink. He'll not be roused."

"So you came to torment me."

"I'll torment you!" She punched me hard enough to take my breath then laughed. I rolled her back into my arms.

Quietly, we lay awhile without speaking. I gently touched the scar on her lip, the tiny scar I loved so much. I kissed her raven hair, her cheek, and was just drifting into a doze when Maude snuggled in for another go. My head immediately began to pulse with an unfamiliar ache. I pushed her away, roughly, for gentle never did it with Maude.

She lay abed kicking the sheet into knots as I dressed and went down the stairs to the second landing. I could hear my master's snores through the walls of the privy, and after emptying my bladder I dared to enter the solar chamber where he slept in his curtained bed.

His clothes hung from a peg next to the bed, his purse still fastened to his cincture. I helped myself to a few coins he would never miss, or if he did, would curse the tavern keeper at last evening's alderman's dinner. My master was not often drunk. Only at celebrations such as the guild feast or an aldermen's dinner, would he drink more than prudent. In this he was like all men, and in it I found no fault. He was, however, a man of high temper, quick to anger and would strike out viciously should he be crossed by an unworthy such as myself. His weapon of choice, a thick walking stick, leaned against his bed, handy to his grasp even then, a standing reminder of past blows delivered to my sorry person. I momentarily retreated from temptation, but in the end thought a bit of extra silver worth the risk. I slipped the coins into my boot.

How I came to be in this man's service is a tale that needs telling, even though the events of that day in 1348 stand apart from it, but not wholly. A man's life is cumulative, after all, building upon itself from the moment of birth. Is that not so? Though I do wonder at times how a man's destiny, so fixed in God's plan, which surely desires the man's salvation, is yet subject to events over which he has little control. Even the narrowest path is littered with crooked stones that will trip the soul, undo it entirely, and send it tumbling down to hell. Yet what child does not begin this perilous journey with less than a sure-footed conviction that the path before him lies straight and smooth to the end?

I was barely eleven years old when I ran from the tin mines in the hope of finding a worthier labor, perhaps with a baker who would fill my belly with bread, or an apothecary who would teach me the magicks of herbs and elixirs; better yet, I saw myself stoking a smithy's furnace or a goldsmith's friendlier fire. Alas, as it sometimes happens in youth, I mistook my daydreams for destiny, and so abandoned my village to seek a larger fortune in a wider world.

But reality came as a hard blow. It was, after all, a time of great hunger. Seasons following seasons of foul weather had caused successive crops to rot in the fields. Country folk who had not enough to feed their families would too often see their children die or be sold for a shilling. No wonder, then, that in exchange for my childish ambitions, I got only thin charity and back-alley beds. Being clumsy in even the simplest tasks besides, no one would keep me in steady employment. Lucky it was that an innkeeper gave me a flask to pee in so I could sell my piss to the wool dyers for a farthing. But for this small kindness, I would have starved.

I still have the flask. It sits in my window with a ribbon tied around the neck. I sometimes fill it with flowers.

"What be your name, boy?" It was the voice of my master speaking to me for the first time. I did not yet know who he was. I looked up into his big face, a massive face it seemed to me then, looming above the filthy hovel near Southwark tannery where I sat huddled against the frigid night air. I had just peed into my flask thinking I would take it to the tanners who use horse urine to cure leather. I had planned to lie, as always, saying that I had crawled under a horse to catch its steaming piss. Then I would use my coin to buy a bun, a hot brown bun, and make it last for two days. But I couldn't fill the flask you see, my bladder and my belly being equally empty. Instead, I looked up into the face of him who would become my master and fainted dead away.

"What be your name, boy?" he asked again after I'd been fed and scrubbed.

"Simon, sir," I answered. Wrapped in a thin bed robe and still shivering from my bath, I stood before a stout table covered with ledgers in a long room hung with rich tapestries and many glowing lamps. The man's skinny wife stood at my back, blocking escape. I would learn in time that the man was an alderman, a person of power in the ward, but even before I knew that, I felt his power over me.

"Where is your village, Simon?"

"Porthtowan, sir."

His eyebrows raised a notch. "Cornwall! You ran away. Why?"

"Well that you ask, sir," I answered readily. "I was the most unfortunate of lads. My father beat me for no trespass. My mother starved me. My brothers tormented me. I could not abide it!"

The alderman thought on my answer, never taking his eyes from my face except to flick a glance at his wife. I felt something pass between them.

His eyes bore into me as he said, "You would have us think you were mistreated when the truth lies in a different place. A wayward lad you are,

Simon; I have no doubt of it. And so too shall I beat you, starve you, and torment you — all that and thrice over if you fail to heed my rules."

I began to protest and got a cuff on the ear for my impudence. The skinny wife had a quick fist. I fell silent, wondering how these strangers knew me so well. I was, for certes, a wayward lad: quick, cunning, and without shame, ever wiggling in and out of mischief. It was my nature, born deep in me.

"Look at me, young Simon," my new master commanded. I looked at him, stared right into his eyes, feigning a courage I did not feel. He said to me without a hint of a kindness, "Things will be different now."

Perhaps it was fatigue from my fruitless travels; perhaps I was simply wiser, but in meeting his hard stare I felt a twisting in my gut that turned the whole of me around. I offered not a word of protest as my life slipped into his hands.

The next morning he kicked me awake from my bed of hemp cloth near the kitchen hearth. "The ward has need of a rat taker. You will do."

I did not take his meaning, rat takers being a thing unheard of in my village, but I didn't like the sound of it at all. I liked it even less when he introduced me to a grizzled man so old his skin dripped like candle melt. "This be Thomas the Rat Taker," my master announced. "He will teach you his occupation."

Thus was I entered into an employment so

rudely different from my own hopes of easy fortune, it took weeks for me to accept it. I think now, I never really did.

I grew to hate my master for his hold over me. Nonetheless, I ate his food, slept by his fire, fetched, and carried. Each morning I followed Old Thomas on his rounds to watch and learn his filthy occupation, all the while devising plans that might free me from my master's charge. But had I not already tried my luck in every village between Porthtown and London? In truth, I got used to not being hungry. My simple occupation was at least purposeful. I felt useful. I felt safe, but most engagingly of all, I lived in the presence of Maude.

My master grunted and rolled over, knocking the walking stick to the floor. I tensed while my thoughts raced to devise an excuse for being so near his bed should he awake. Luckily, the stick landed on a coverlet that had slipped off the bed, muting its fall. I backed away not breathing until I was outside the room.

Maude was sleeping when I returned to the attic. The bed robe lay twisted about her body, caught between her legs and only half covering her nakedness. One breast was fully exposed; the other covered teasingly just above the nipple. Ah, my Maude! Everything about her was wanton, from her bare arms out-flung to her raven hair spread across the pillow. Dark, sharp, and dangerous she was, a rapier aimed always at my heart.

Older than I, yet she, too, was a child when we first met.

My master had purchased her at a country fair from a widowed mother who could not feed her. He had brought her home to attend to his wife who was ailing. At first, she rarely glanced at me, and when she did, it was with eyes full of knowing beyond her years. Much later I came to understand that look, but at the time I believed that her shadowed gaze held only the measure of her disdain for my sorry person. I tiptoed in her presence, made myself small in an attempt to look at her without being seen. I loved her even then. Hopelessly, as I do to this day, but in secret, for Maude did not believe in love. Had I ever revealed to her the fullness in my heart, she would have laughed at my simplicity.

Maude stretched beneath the sheet, pulling the robe to expose fully her tempting breast. Her eyes opened and she reached for me as her lips curled into a naughty smile. She had been awake all the while. I took her in my arms, lifted her free of the cot, and carried her down the stairs to the master's bed. The old man slept on, drooling into his pillow. I released her gently with a soft kiss. She did not cling, but simply laid back and watched me leave. And that's how the master found her sometime later, lying naked beside him. As I made ready to leave the house, I heard her scream, but for pain or for pleasure I could not say. Pain and pleasure were all one in the same for my Maude.

Simon describes his first sighting of rats mysteriously dead

Carrying my trowel, gloves, traps, bait and poisons inside my carcass bag, I stepped outside the third floor window and onto the ladder that led down to the alley. The church bells had ceased ringing, their riotous peels giving way to the cries of fishmongers and other sellers of food and fripperies. The shrill clamor of too many voices out of tune jarred my already edgy spirits. My head again began to throb with sharp intensity, forcing me to pause in my descent. I pressed my forehead against the ladder rail, my eyes screwed shut, and breathed through open lips. As I clung there, quite unable to trust my feet to find the next rung down, I heard footsteps below. I slowly twisted to glance over my shoulder.

The gate in the neighbor's garden wall swung open and out stepped a servant maid carrying a market basket. She glanced up at me and smiled. "God be with you, Master Rat Taker," she said with a curtsy meant only to mock me, then swept down the alley and turned onto Thames Street, leaving her master's gate ajar.

Her name was Alyce, I remember now, a maid of no more than fifteen years, with a pert tongue and a wide, flirtatious smile. Alyce was one of three servants employed by the wealthy vintner who lived behind the wall. Her family, to whom she returned each night, lived in Farringdon Ward. Her brothers, both cobblers, would come each evening to walk her home, for it was a goodly way to go. That she had many suitors I had no doubt. Unlike my Maude, who was wild as mustard, Alyce possessed subtle, more domestic charms that invited confidences and made young men dream of cradles.

Alyce and her entire family were among the first taken by the pestilence that was to besiege the city. That is why, seeing her again through the eyes of memory, I feel a sadness that I no way felt on that morning. At that time, not knowing her unhappy fate, I saw her only as a careless maid who had left her master's gate ajar.

I continued down the ladder, slowly, to spare my aching head. When I reached bottom, a dog barked, sending a flurry of crows up and over the vintner's wall. As I watched the flock ascend to the sky, a longing for the moor where I had, as a child, flushed so many birds from the scrub pierced me to the quick. For a brief moment, I was there again on the moor, only to return in a dizzying rush to the place where I stood watching city crows flying over London rooftops like bits of char in the wind. I almost climbed the ladder and went back to bed, and may have done so but for the sudden appearance of Pye charging down the alley with a rattail hanging through her teeth.

Heedless of her momentum, the dog flung herself into my arms. Despite the stab of pain this impact delivered to my head, I laughed out loud at her reckless exuberance. She was an ancient breed, born to flush game: short-legged, sturdy and high-strung. Even when standing still she looked busy. That was Pye. I opened my carcass bag and she dropped in her prize as her tail whipped the air. Her eyes looked up at me, bright with intelligence and demanding praise. I could smell rat on her warm breath, but I didn't mind. We understood each other, both of us being ratters, me by circumstance, and she by nature. I have to say I coveted that hound. We would have made good industry together.

A rude command issued from the vintner's garden. "Pye! Return, bitch!" A moment later Amaury Swain, the vintner's apprentice and, more enviably to my mind, Pye's master, stepped into the alley. Upon seeing me, he halted; his back stiffened. "Come, girl!" he commanded again, not taking his eyes from me. "Come, I say."

The dog made a dash for the open gate, stopped just short of entering and returned to me, barking playfully. Amaury grimaced. "Pye!

You wayward hound! Come here to me or I shall break your bones."

Pye ran back. Amaury made a grab for her collar, but she eluded him and came to me again. I knelt on one knee and opened my arms. Pye flew into them, knocking me over completely. My trowel, carcass bag and gloves went flying. Never mind. I embraced her warmly as she licked my chin, cheeks, nose with her moist, sinuous tongue.

Amaury yanked us apart. I stared up into his angry eyes. They seemed unduly angry, I thought, for I had made no trespass.

"Ho, Amaury," I said with forced cheer. "Why so sharpish? You be as sour as your master's wine this morn."

"I like you not, Rat Taker, this or any morn. The sight of you sours my day."

Truth, I did not like him either. Amaury was not a likable fellow. I did my best to discomfort him, such that I could from my lowly station. A better man would have laughed me away, but Amaury was proud beyond good sense, an easy mark for my jibes.

We were of similar age and stature, Amaury and I. We both stood taller than was common, both still bore the chiseled look of youth, but, in fairness, Amaury was by far the handsomer. His short, well-cut padded jacket showed off his lean figure to good advantage. His large almond eyes caused even Maude to make remark, calling them beautiful. She fancied, too, his crow-black hair that curled womanish about his face. I, of course, saw only a mouth too quick to sneer, a nose too high in the air.

To Amaury, I was a churlish lout. We were natural enemies.

"Did you open the master's gate?" he spat.

"I did not open the gate," I said, rising to my feet. "And you must learn to control your beast with a playful hand, Amaury. She'll not willingly fly into your fist."

His nose quivered with annoyance. Holding Pye by the scruff with one hand, he gave her collar a yank with the other. She resisted.

"And a God's good morning to you," I muttered insincerely. Exiting the alley, I rounded onto Thames Street. As soon as I passed the vintner's house, I gave a long, high whistle and held it until Pye came bounding around the corner. I broke into a run, still whistling. She followed hot on my heels. Neither of us paid the slightest heed to the string of curses issuing from the alley.

The street rakers had passed through Thames Street only moments before, leaving the gutters passably clean, but the air was already thickening with gaseous vapors blowing off the polluted river. I tell you, verily, London stinks. Add to the rude smell an equally rude citizenry picking their way through lanes most often clotted with dung, offal, and other recognizable but unspeakable filth and you will have a fair description of an afternoon stroll through the city. On this day, a dead horse lying across a main intersection, threatened to compound the offense. A street raker was sawing the beast into parts to make moving it easier. A rivulet of blood coursed the length of Thames Street and trickled down side lanes. There was no escaping it.

Pye, of course, was in ecstasy, sniffing every dung heap and scummy puddle in our path. I could no way hurry her, even though I had looped the cord from my carcass bag through her collar and tugged persistently to move her forward. Alas, her strength of purpose surpassed mine, so our passage was exasperatingly slow — until she smelled a rat.

The first one crossed our path as we approached the wharf. Pye took off swift as a bow-shot, pulling the leash taut, almost wrenching it from my grasp. I ran behind and nearly pitched over when she stopped short and turned back whimpering. She would go no farther, even though the fleeing rat was still in sight. I could see no cause for her behavior, nothing barred her chase, but forward she would not go. The rat disappeared under a stack of kegs behind a tavern.

Then I spotted two others lying within a clogged drain directly in our path, both dead, their bodies oddly twisted yet still supple. Black blood oozed from their noses and even from a distance I could smell the cloying stench of death. I held my breath as I scraped up the bodies with my trowel and dropped them into my bag, adding yet another stink to my morning.

Pye tugged to be away, but this time it was I who refused to budge. I held her on a short leash while I scanned the area for other vermin, dead or alive, or for poisons that might explain how the two rats had died. Several minutes of poking about offered no clues. I started to move on when the door of the Red Rooster banged open and a voice called.

"Ratiker!"

I spun around to find the tavern keeper Thomas Penyman, a most surly fellow, thick and squat as an ale keg, standing on the stoop of his establishment. His sour expression remindful of the ale he served. He motioned me to follow him into the tavern.

Without a word, he lit a candle stump, ushered me through the keg room and down the steps into a cellar that reeked of a corruption I readily recognized. Pye, though quivering to explore the cellar's depths, obeyed my command and remained on the upper landing. The candlelight flickered in a draft from a source unseen. Somewhere in the cellar a door stood open.

"Open doors give rats easy passage," I commented.

"It's that saucy maid again," the tavern keeper snorted. He abandoned me to the dark while he went in search of the open door. I heard a slam and the thump of a lowered bar, then he returned with something sly playing around his lips. The expression vanished when he caught my eye. "She escapes to some secret hole in the earth to tryst with her lover," he explained. "Returns late and breathless; leaves the door ajar."

"Often?"

"Often enough. Someday she will lose herself underground. I'll have to hire another maid. Not so pretty next time."

Not a happy fate half-wished on the maid; not one I could accept even in jest, for I knew well the underground passages that ran beneath the city.

They are still there, these years later, those tunnels beneath our feet, only less remembered now. Were the citizens of London aware of these ancient passages filled with the rubble of ruins and catacombs, they could pass, as I often did, from the Tower Gate to St. Paul's without ever seeing the light of day. But few would want to do that, not now, not then, which is why I would often see my own footprints coming and going in the powdery dust. A wonder it is that I never got lost in that maze.

Truth is, I often came close to getting lost. I was young and eager for the adventure my unfortunate occupation denied me. The underground was for me a splendid escape. At times, after emptying and resetting traps, I would venture deep into those subterranean halls until my lamp burned dangerously low. With not a soul to hear my cries or my pounding on dead-end walls, I would at last stumble into a chamber I recognized. Then with great relief would I enter the house above where a giggling maid would let me pass through the door to daylight. Once I startled an unwary servant by appearing in his master's cellar seemingly out of nowhere. He accosted me, fearing me a thief until I showed him the contents of my carcass bag. "Damn fool!" he said tossing me to the ground. "Why don't you mark your route?" The next day I purchased a lump of chalk to mark a trail along the passage walls allowing me to explore even farther.

Aye, familiar am I with that underground, that secret place where the rats of London thrive. Yet I say no more of it for fear of touching too soon on events that, when my resolve grows stronger, will turn the fearful light of memory on that place where my life fell into an abyss.

Penyman used his candle to light an oil lamp hanging from a low beam. I went immediately to attend the traps I had set three days past. The cellar ran long and narrow. The hard earthen floor was always slick with spillage, although spaces between the fat kegs provided reasonably dry nesting spots for the brown rats seeking environments near water and refuse dumps. The wharf with its many old establishments was for them a perfect neighborhood.

I remember Old Thomas asking on our first day together, "What know you of rats?"

"What is there to know?" I had responded dismissively.

"Well, first off, they be smarter than you."

I had scoffed at that, but experience has proven Old Thomas more right than I dare to admit. Rats are indeed intelligent creatures. They seek only the freshest food and water and quickly learn what foods make them sick.

Poisons, which I happily sold upon request, are of little use, for rats know to avoid them. The old man taught me to set traps with strips of white cloth, dry grasses and other materials suitable for nest building and to place them in dark corners with the spring catch facing the wall. Older rats avoid even these, but younger, less experienced ones, are often drawn in. The truest method for ridding a building of vermin is to keep them out altogether by blocking every means of entrance, but many of London's cellars are too open to the underground tunnels. Thus were my efforts both futile and never ending, keeping me in good labor.

I emptied two of the traps in Penyman's cellar, one containing a mouse, the other, a fat brown rat that should have known better. Then I set all the traps in new locations, finding as I did so, three black rats, or ship rats as some call them, bearing similar death signs as those on the wharf: bodies oddly contorted, oozing blood, a putrid smell of death.

"Did you set out a new poison?" I asked the tavern keeper.

Penyman looked at me with clear disgust. "That be your job, Rat Taker. What are you saying? Your poison didn't kill these vermin?"

I shook my head. "Nay, these three died from something unknown to me."

He shrugged. It made no difference to him how they died. I took the candle and searched the corners again, hearing the scratch of feet scurrying away from the flickering light. I found one nest containing four hairless young. I scooped them and the nest into my carcass bag. I then sprinkled a few sprigs of dry fleabane on the floor and set them aflame to ward off the ever-persistent fleas.

Pye whimpered at the top of the cellar stair, eager to be off. I shouldered my bag and followed the tavern keeper up to the landing. "Boil some herbs down here to clean out the stink," I said.

"Aye," the man answered as he pushed Pye out of his way.

"And have your goodwife burn a measure of fleabane in the corners every day. That may save you some discomfort from fleabites."

He growled. We were now standing in the taproom. A pretty maid was drawing off pitchers of ale without spilling a drop. She looked a juicy morsel with pink, pouty lips. I envisioned her in the arms of her lover and envied the man.

Penyman grunted a distracted dismissal as he

ushered me out the door, and I knew he would forget about the fleabane as soon as I was gone.

I always burned a bit of fleabane after cleaning my traps; it was part of my service, but in truth, it was more a courtesy than a cure. Fleas are harder to kill than rats. They abandon dead vermin and jump on the next living body that comes near, which very often is the rat taker. This I learned early when I was new to the occupation and crazed with bites grown pustulant from my incessant scratching. Finally, Old Thomas took pity and shared a secret.

"Wrap yourself in horsehide," he had confided. "Fleas don't like it." How he knew this I cannot say for the man never said much beyond the necessary. I knew he had traveled in distant lands, returning with knowledge for riches, but I never learned where he traveled or why and only occasionally did I benefit from his hoard of information.

I followed his advice and petitioned my master for funds to buy a horse. The horse trader that sold me the nag, already half-dead before I killed her, never knew my purpose for buying. He thought I was dotty, no doubt, but I got the best of that bargain. The nag provided a bounty of hide that I took to the tanners to make supple. My master's wife was still living then. She cut and stitched the hide into a number of useful articles: straps to brace my hose, gloves, cap and vest, slippers for my shoes and a carcass sack. Maude called these articles my "nellies" because Nellie is what I named the old horse before I cut her throat. I cannot say I never had another fleabite, but far fewer than expected given my occupation.

Thomas Penyman was scratching his ribs when I stepped out his door, prompting me to say once again, "Fleabane! Don't forget. And God be with you!" He returned to his trade without answering and died within the week — he, his wife, two sons, and the pretty maid — without my ever seeing any of them again. The city wardens boarded up the tavern, but too late.

From the Journal of Jonathan Purchell
30 March, Anno Domini 1375

In the matter of Simon's recollections, our routine has fallen into a simple pattern.

He comes to my room on occasional evenings after my daytime duties are complete. He comes always unannounced so that I wait each night for his footfall on the attic stair, holding sleep at bay until my lamp sputters and I give in to weariness. When he does come, I go silently to my table, dip a newly sharpened quill in the inkpot, and wait while he sits on my bed staring into space, selecting memories. When at last he speaks, the words come out rehearsed, but rough and tangled for all that. I edit as I write, though at times when the meaning is not clear I copy verbatim. Later, after he has left, I untangle the meaning and write the pages anew. It is tedious work, but I am trained to it and I take pride in my skill.

The room in which I work is no more than a cubby beneath the attic eaves with space only for a straw mattress on a narrow cot, a small writing table, a three-legged stool, and a chamber pot. The beamed ceiling slants down to within four feet of the floor at the outside wall. There is no window. I have but one hook at the foot of my bed on which to hang clothes. The space that accommodates my table and stool is also at the foot of the bed: crammed tightly under the dormer so that the hanging oil lamp continually bumps my head. The stool straddles a threshold without a door. I enter and exit the house by a ladder accessed through a window at the end of a passage outside my room.

This miserly cubby, in which I cannot even stretch my legs to full, is all he affords me, this and an equally miserly pittance with which I buy my own food and necessities. Apart from his counting room, which I enter and exit from the front courtyard, I have never been invited into any other part of the house.

It is an imposing house. During my first visit, the day he hired me, I noted that it had four levels: kitchen, and counting room on the ground level, the solar, sleeping alcove and privy on the first level, and, as I suspected yet did not know for certain, an attic on the third. During my interview I learned of the cellar where he stores samples of his trade and what else I know not. The house impressed me that first day, and I could imagine myself well positioned were I in service to Simon Ratiker.

He greeted me at the front door with a hearty thump on my back. "Good day, good day!" he said, his eyes twinkling with good will, or so it seemed. I had dressed in my best hose and tunic, careful to stitch under the frayed edges of my sleeves. I would not have him believe I was impoverished and desperate for employment, though in fact that was the case. Had I not entered the man's service, I would have probably died of hunger that very night. I was rescued from so early a demise by Simon's hospitality. I nearly fainted with gratitude when he invited me to share his dinner of thick bean soup, pork pasty, and sweetmeats served hot from a tavern across the street. It took all my self-control not to devour my plate; but, aware of being watched, I forced myself to take small bites at a leisurely pace and to leave some food untouched. The wine went down easily as well. From his own cellars, he said, and he asked my opinion of it. Knowing nothing of wine, I merely nodded agreeably.

Our conversation was rambling, a sharing of histories and local news. He asked about my qualifications as a clerk, but he seemed most interested in personal anecdotes. He acted as a man starving for social converse so I played free with my memories, if only in gratitude for the fine meal. I now know he was testing to see if my manner of expression pleased him. It was my choice of words that interested him.

"You are a quick lad," he said at last, leaning back from his plate. He had made his decision. I braced myself for a declaration that could mean my salvation or my doom. He surprised me. "Return on Monday to begin your duties," he said evenly. "My last clerk left three weeks ago for family reasons, and there is much catching up to do."

"How much wage can I expect?" I asked as boldly as I dared. He looked at me sharp, as if the question surprised him. He then raised his eyes to the rafters and pulled on his lower lip, appearing to give the question deep thought. One would have supposed he had not considered the matter at all before that moment. I almost ventured to ask what he paid his last clerk, thinking that a good bargaining place to begin, but he at last slid his eyes back to me and named a sum shockingly low.

Disappointment robbed me of breath so that I could not immediately reply. Finally, I said, almost whispered, "That is not enough. Can you not offer more?"

He suddenly looked as crestfallen as I. It was a sad moment for us both. Then he brightened, "I have it! I'll give you free lodging in a small room in the attic. It's being used for naught and it would suit me to have you so nearby.

"And," he raced on before I could respond, "some evenings, after you finish the accounts, you could help me record my recollections. An uncommon duty, I know," he added when he saw my surprise. "'Tis a mere fancy I would indulge for amusement, not for the world to read. I thought to undertake the labor myself, but I desire it to be true and well-fashioned, and alas, the task surpasses my skill." He paused and studied his hands, which lay palms down on the table, then said, "For this extra work, I would add five pence to your wages and count it well worth it." He looked up at me and smiled as if he had just offered the world. "How say you?" he urged when he saw my hesitation.

I had no choice. The offer of a room seemed generous. Although I was loath to leave my small lodgings on Grace Church Street, the saving in rent would be considerable. I did not ask how much work his dictations would require, nor did I ask to see the attic room. I was desperate.

He poured me a half-cup of wine to seal the bargain then sat smiling as he watched me drink. The second I lowered the empty cup he ushered me out the front door with more nods and smiles. My foot had barely touched the stoop when the door slammed shut at my back. I walked on, feeling optimistic for the first time in weeks.

But I was deceived and am so still I fear. Apart from the man's miserly ways and vacant heart, there is something twisted in this house: something is askew that niggles my mind yet eludes detection. The secret lies in the man, methinks, and wants exposing. I sit now in the sputtering light of my abusive lamp and contemplate a course of discovery.

In veritate scribo,
Johannes P.

Simon further describes his morning rounds

Every London ward is plagued with vermin, but the wards beyond the Vintnery were not my concern. My ward, being located so near the River Thames, kept me busy enough. Although the Vintnery is a small ward compared to the others, its citizens number themselves among the most prosperous and their houses among the grandest in the city. Yet rodents thrive within the cellars of those houses as easily as in the meanest cottage.

Pye walked ahead, nose to the ground, straining at the leash, as I continued my rounds. Margaret Fletcher of Fish Street, twice widowed and again remarried in spite of her sharpish tongue, met me at her kitchen door.

"Well that you came, Rat Taker, and about time, too. The smell of one of your dead rats or something equally foul is polluting my house. The odor comes from behind the cistern wall. Get you to it now."

She treated Pye to a bowl of scraps while I went into the cellar. As she had said, a rat had trapped itself in the cistern enclosure and had died there. I thanked the heavens that it had not fallen into Lady Margaret's water supply, though it could have happened so easily it was only a matter of time before it did. As I left, I bade the lady to get a tighter cover for her cistern.

Next, little Roger Jacob, Master Jacob's youngest son, admitted me to his father's house. Mercer Jacob, a wealthy draper, followed me around cautioning where not to set my traps lest his son mistake one for a toy.

An unhappy man was Mercer Jacob. "It's all this talk of pestilence! Very bad," he lamented with much wringing of his hands. "Folk are avoiding the shops, the market stalls and other public places. If the sickness does invade the city, I fear customers will stop coming altogether. I may be forced to close my shop, and then where will I be?"

Of course, he predicted true; but when the pestilence did finally force the shops and stalls to close, it no longer mattered to Mercer Jacob.

Aye, and I did find more rats mysteriously dead in both houses, so that after leaving Mercer Jacob's, I made it a point to investigate every house that would allow me entry. In one garden I encountered a rat right out in the open running in circles, crying aloud most piteously before it fell into violent convulsions. I killed it simply out of pity.

"Rats are God's creatures, too," I recall old

Thomas saying. "In time they will earn a measure of your respect."

"And a measure of my pity." I ventured.

"Why is that?"

"Because though they be God's creatures, they are so commonly reviled."

"Spare your pity. Rats are indeed reviled, but in that they have an advantage over you and me. Rats do not know they are despised."

All the same, on that morning I felt pity. Spring traps are sure and swift; but this rat was in a long agony, and so I killed it with my trowel.

My carcass bag became uncommonly heavy before the end of morning. It caused a stench so high a crowd of schoolboys returning home for dinner surrounded me in a narrow lane, holding their noses while hurling jibes. Pye started into a frenzy of barks, adding to the commotion. I swung the bag in a circle above my head pretending that I would soon let it fly into the boys' midst and befoul them with its contents. The boys scampered off, screaming. Neighbors came to their windows. Shopkeepers watched from their stalls. A passerby nailed me with a hard stare. I hurried on, feeling none the better for my harmless ploy.

Luckily, my headache began to wane sometime earlier, though I couldn't say when, nor would I now mention it except that before returning to my master's house for dinner, I made one last stop at St. Michael Paternoster, where once again my head began to throb with new intensity.

Father Liam greeted me just outside the nave. "Where come by you to such a fine companion?" he asked, his eyes bright with amusement. He knew Amaury and of the enmity between us, and most surely he recognized the man's dog.

"Borrowed," I said. "She's a ratter. Like me."

"Ah! Well, then," he said, leading the way," bring her along." I followed him down the pillared aisle that lined the nave. This front section of the church was, as usual, filled with citizens conducting trade or social converse. Their voices and the echo of their voices rose to the vaulted ceiling. Nonetheless, the sound of Pye's toenails click-clicking against the paved floor caused heads to turn. Father Liam glanced back without breaking his stride. "Will the hound be making confession?" he asked aloud. All those within earshot chuckled at the near blasphemy.

I loved Father Liam, a small, thoughtful man who laughed easily and was kind to men of every station. He appeared delicate, but there was in him a strength both physical and spiritual that commanded the respect of even the most wayward parishioner. When I was a lad newly come to my master's house, Father Liam one day found me in the corner of an empty chapel. I was crying over some abuse I cannot now remember. He approached me slowly, holding out his hand as he would for a strange dog to sniff. I reached for him instinctively. He drew me into his arms and held me, as a true father would, until my crying ceased. He then let me go without a word.

Now, as we entered a stairwell in the South Transept where he unlocked the door to the crypt, I reached for him again. "Father Liam," I said, clutching his sleeve, "I am troubled. No, not to confess. I feel . . . all day there has been something . . ." My headache throbbed dully behind my eyes. I leaned into the wall and rested my head against the cool stone, seeking relief.

"Apprehension?"

"Apprehension," I repeated without moving, "What is that?"

He thought for a moment then said, "Fear of what's expected." He waited. When I did not reply, he said, "We are all feeling it. The pestilence will soon be at our gates and we'll not be able to keep it out." He shook his head in lament before lifting his eyes toward the sanctuary and, making the Sign, descended into the crypt.

Holding Pye by her makeshift leash, I followed the priest into the silent, tomblike vault where bare altars lined the walls, each awaiting in somber silence the next Mass for the Dead. Stone sarcophagi, some carved with effigies, stood in rows beneath the main altar in the church above. Three torch lamps cast fitful shadows against the walls and low ceiling. The heady scent of sanctity, of incense and candle melt, lingered in cool air.

Quickly I went about resetting traps while Pye sniffed in corners. Father Liam stood apart, whispering prayers for the souls enshrined within that cold, timeless place.

St. Michael's is but a stone's throw from my master's house. In fact, a passage runs through my master's cellar and beyond to where it dead-ends against the crypt wall. It is a wide, well-timbered passage that must have been created during the church's construction. St. Michael Paternoster is an old church, and the walls of the foundation were disintegrating. For years, cracks in the more distressed areas were giving rats passage into the crypt. As a precaution, I had laid traps in the tunnels leading to the church and had mortared over all the cracks I could find. Now rats were dying strangely throughout the ward, and I did not want their vile corpses contaminating the church. The idea of it disturbed me. I began another inspection around the walls.

Pye's eager whine alerted me to a find: a crack in the wall abutting the underground passage leading to my Master's cellar. I had seen it months earlier when it was inconsequential, but now it had widened beneath the weight of the building. Father Liam came to look as well, "Ah!" he said. "But surely it is too small."

I shook my head. "They can squeeze through a hole smaller than a farthing. I'll mortar it up this very day."

"You provide good service," Father Liam said

kindly.

His words took me by surprise. Few people ever said a kind word to me. Oddly, Father Liam's comment served only to remind me of how lacking in kind words my life was.

"It is a no man's service," I replied bitterly.

"How is that?"

"No man wishes to do it, so the charge falls to a 'no man' such as I."

Father Liam looked at me in long silence. I had time to regret my words before he spoke again. I did not want him to think me guilty of self-pity.

"Simon," he said quietly, "sit with me awhile."

He led me to a marble bench especially installed for a long-ago visiting bishop no one now remembered. Once seated, Father Liam gazed at the Crucifix above the main altar as if listening. He then bowed his head to pray. "Oh, Lord Jesus Christ, who in your Humanity, art No Man and Sin Taker of the world, hear our prayer. In this time of Great Tribulation, we ask that Thou deliver us from the suffering that does overwhelm our spirits and threaten our faith. Yet, if that be not possible, we pray that our sorrows be made one with you who suffered for our sins. Willingly we do offer our suffering unto Thee so that, with all men, we may share in the work of your Redeeming Sacrifice and thus share in the world's redemption. Amen."

I knew the prayer, as did every member of the

parish for we had recited it often during the days of famine. Now it was plague, not famine, which threatened our lives and caused folk to fear for their souls. It was hard not to be afraid, for if God did send plagues and famines as a retribution for our sins, as was generally believed, then our sins were surely immeasurable. What hope did any of us have for salvation?

Father Liam had no such fears. "In times of great suffering we must award to suffering a great purpose," he told us. "And it is this. Through our pain, we are redeemers with Christ. Through our pain, we are redeemed in Him. This is the holy symmetry of our salvation."

He pursed his lips then smiled and turned to me. "Joy and well-being are gifts from God. But sorrow is God's gift, too. Embrace it gracefully for it is the work of the cross in which we have been given a noble part. From our deepest cry to our smallest tear, nothing is wasted. Believe that, Simon, when you feel bitter about your station."

I wanted to believe, but I did not understand.

"To want to believe is enough," Father Liam said. "The Lord will do the rest."

Would that I had taken his words to heart, but not knowing of the trial in store for me that very day, I quickly forgot them. Now, in my time of remembering, I do regret how easily, how carelessly, I did forget.

Father Liam overpaid me for my contract to mortar the crack, though he had no need to.

Sealing cracks was part of my service, but I accepted the bonus gratefully, knowing it would buy a silk ribbon for Maude.

Finished with my morning rounds, I made haste for home, thinking to ease my headache with a brew of betony before taking dinner with Maude.

Pye, too, was happy to return to her master's house, as happy as she had been to leave; such is the way with hounds. I let her in through the vintner's gate, and she ran to the door barking urgently. Maid Alyce admitted her almost at once then scowled at me from the open door. "Amaury is very cross with you for stealing Pye," she scolded. "Now here you are stealing roses from the master's garden!"

"Come now, Alyce, the vintner will never miss a few buds." My fist was already full of red blooms and I was cutting another with my knife. The yard behind my master's house boasted no such beauties. I knew Maude would think them a treat.

"Plantagenet roses," Alyce informed me, stepping prettily into the garden. "Summer's last, and he will miss them, mark me. 'Tis a rose finest among the fine and he counts the buds every evening." She was smiling, being only half serious, but when she drew nearer her face twisted in disgust. "Ugh! What a stink, Rat Taker! Go you. Get out before you wilt the grass!" She shooed me out the gate with her skirt, showing a

bit of under linen and well-shaped legs. I winked
at her and closed the gate behind me.

From the Journal of Jonathan Purchell
24 March, Anno Domini 1375

A curious thing has happened that has firmed my resolve to pursue the mystery of Simon Ratiker, not that his recollections, as yet unrevealing, haven't already deepened my curiosity. Today there came more.

It happened at the haberdasher's stall in the marketplace where I regularly buy quills and ink. Three students of law stood ahead of me, giving me time to look over the merchandise, trying on caps, fingering strands of lace. Meanwhile I listened as the men talked about their prospects after completing their examinations, which I gathered would be soon. Mostly they bragged. My attention began to drift until I heard one say, ". . . and if not, I'll be gone to Ratiker, for certes." I spun around in time to see the clerk caution the speaker with his eyes as he jerked his head in my direction. Two of the young men turned to stare at me while the third made his purchase. They left hurriedly, the third man glancing at me as he swept down the street.

I took my turn at the counter where the proprietor busied himself squaring off Italian-made papers, too dear for my purse, all the while avoiding my eyes.

"What is the meaning of 'gone to Ratiker'?" I asked.

He shrugged. "Five quills. One block of ink," he mumbled, adding them up.

"Surely you know," I persisted, making no move to pay. He looked at me then. "You are clerk to Simon Ratiker, are you not?"

"Aye."

"There have been others."

"I know that."

"They come and then they go more suddenly than when they came. When they go, they never come back."

"Master Simon is not the most generous of employers," I explained. "I myself have vowed that as soon as I have saved enough to buy a presentable tunic, I will seek employment elsewhere. Sometimes you must take what is offered until a better opportunity arises."

"There you have it!" he said with obvious relief. "That is all it means: to take what is offered. That is all. It is not a shameful thing, verily."

"My employer's ways are known in the city?" I inquired.

"Nay. The man is a mystery, but perhaps not to you." He waited expectantly for what gossip I would share, his nose fairly twitching. A sudden, perverse loyalty to my employer took me by surprise. I paid my reckoning and left without saying another word. I decided then and there that I would never return.

I dislike my employer. Have I not said so? But a slur against him is a slur against me. I had gone to Ratiker because I could do no better. That was the implication. For hours after, I felt the sting of it. I thought of little else, so that only much later did I recall what more the haberdasher had said: "They go more suddenly than when they came. When they go they never come back." Unaccountably, the words made me shudder.

For certes, there have been former clerks. How many I could

not say, but I had seen at least two different scripts in this year's ledger. One at the beginning of the book went to the end of January. Another appeared two months later, going almost to the time of my hire. A rather quick changeover, I grant you, but unusually so? I begin to wonder.

In veritate scribo,
Johannes P.

Simon tells of an unhappy discovery

Maude waved from the kitchen door as I entered my master's gates. I closed the gate and waved back, concealing the roses from view. Often did I surprise her with notions: a ribbon, a thimble, a twist of thread. But a rose was rare. I delighted in the pleasure my simple gifts gave to her. In truth, the pleasure was always more mine. Her smile of surprise, her kiss of gratitude, gave me the feeling, however counterfeit, of what other men must feel when they are loved.

I stepped into the yard as Maude went back into the kitchen.

It was well past the dinner hour, having spent an unusually long time on my morning rounds. Although my headache robbed me of appetite, I looked forward to eating in the yard with Maude, just the two of us as always. My master ate his noon meal with friends in a tavern. When he did not, he ate alone in his tapestried room where I was not allowed to enter until I had stripped off my horsehide nellies and washed my hands.

I did not go directly into the house, wanting

first to unload my carcass bag. I rounded to the far end of the yard to a deep pit lined with stones and quicklime, dumped the contents of my bag, then covered everything with more quicklime, water, and a layer of dirt. On that day, I remember, because the stench was high, I shoveled in extra layers of earth, making sure that the corpses were sufficiently buried while the quicklime did its work. The pit was hedged round with boxwoods, their branches plashed and neatly pruned, hiding the pit from view of the house. All the supplies I needed — shovel, pail, quicklime, sand, and cistern — were stored in a small shed that backed against the garden wall. This corner of the garden was mine to maintain and I kept it neat. Unfortunately, the rest of the yard was so ill kept the hedge drew your eye, ever reminding you of the pit and its contents.

I had just chunked the shovel into the mound of dirt when I heard footsteps in the alley. The vintner's gate opened then closed. Someone from that house was returning home. Seconds later Pye barked joyously and I could hear her running down the graveled path, another bark followed by a soft impact. Someone let out a grunt and a breathless laugh. It was Amaury. Returning from where, I wondered. Pye barked again, softly, as if assuring her master that her sally with the rat taker was a thing forgotten, that she was glad to be home.

I felt suddenly bereft, as if abandoned by a

trusted friend. Foolish I was to covet her. Animals, people, they know to whom they belong and love belonging too deeply to stray far. Those of us who belong to no one can only stand aside and try to understand. Nonetheless, I believed I appreciated Pye more than Amaury ever could. We had an interest in common, she and I, but she was not and never would be my dog.

My mind slid into thoughts of Amaury, to his angry face glaring down at me in the alley. How was it I riled the man so, I who had nothing while he had the entire world before him? From whence came his anger toward me, a mere bug beneath his shoe? I had always put it down to his pride, but that did not satisfy. Consider our differences, if only for a moment, and you will understand my perplexity.

Amaury was a man of station, a son of wealth yet wholly dedicated to the mysteries of his trade. He had responsibilities to his family, to his master, and to himself, all of which he took seriously. He had mastered the subtleties of wine and was nearing the end of his apprenticeship. With the help of his family, he looked to establish his own wine shop, to become a member of a powerful guild, to import and sell the wines that England demanded, to marry well and grow fat. In truth, I envied his prospects while despising his competence.

I, on the other hand, had no station at all. I was but one of my master's charities, a good deed he stored away as a hedge against hellfire or as a stepping stone into heaven, depending on how close to the line he was on any particular day. Neither he nor any man cared about who I was. I lived unencumbered by other men's ambitions, was blessed with an unaccountable freedom, but it was a freedom unexplored. Limited by inexperience, I could not yet discern the possibilities; so I speak of this as one looking back and seeing what I could not see then.

All of this aside, I can now admit to what I would not admit at the time, that the true source of the dislike between Amaury and myself was not the difference in our station or the fickle loyalties of his hound. What set me against him and he against me was our mutual interest in Maude.

I had long suspected that Amaury had feelings for Maude, but was never certain until one morning in Cheapside where Maude and I had gone together: she to shop, I to complete an errand for my master. We had no sooner parted with a plan to reunite at the market cross than I noticed Amaury among the marketgoers. Avoiding an encounter that was sure to spoil my morning, I ducked out of sight and waited for him to pass.

Standing in the shadows between two stalls, I saw him spy Maude and change direction to cross her path; I watched him idly reach for a pear on the cart from which she was making a purchase. Saw him feign surprise upon catching her eye. Maude returned his greeting with an open smile. They spoke. Maude laughed at something he said. He looked down and grinned at his pointed shoes, pleased that she had caught his meaning. Then Maude made a quick remark and they both laughed with genuine merriment. They never touched. In fact they stood well apart. Just two neighbors, they were, enjoying a friendly encounter.

Maude said good-bye. I watched Amaury watch her leave, his arms dangling, his hand still holding the pear. He stood immobile, buffeted by marketgoers until she was out of sight. The man was besotted. I would have felt smug had I not known too well what he was feeling. I am now sure, yes, I am quite sure, it was in that moment I began to truly hate the apprentice. I wondered if Maude knew he fancied her, but feared to ask the question that would put her wise if she did not. I feared equally her answer if she did, so I never asked. In the end, I had no need to.

All of that was in the past and out of mind as I washed the worst of the stink off me at the well then stepped through the kitchen door. I held the roses before me.

The room was bathed in sunlight streaming through open shutters. Maud's back was to me as she ladled steaming broth from the iron pot. A tray set with cheese, fruit and two meat pies from the bakery sat on the dining board. A glazed pitcher standing beside the tray glowed in the autumn light. It was to break a man's heart, so exquisite was that sunny moment until Maude, holding a steaming bowl in each hand, turned and saw the roses. Her eyes went wide and she stopped too short. The steaming broth slopped over the sides of the bowls onto her fingers and she dropped both bowls on the slab floor. Broth splattered in every direction. The hem of her gown and the entire front of her apron were stained with it. "Simon," she whispered, staring at the red blooms, "What have you done?"

I lifted my eyes from the mess at my feet, ready to laugh away the mishap, when I saw of a sudden a flask balanced on the window ledge. In it stood the finest rose from the finest of the fine: a Plantagenet. The single bloom, so purposefully plucked from among all the others, declared the very depths of one man's heart, and did so far more eloquently than the careless handful I offered.

Maude followed my gaze then turned back to me, her eyes challenging me to make remark.

A driving pain pierced my head, searing hot and red behind my eyes. I staggered into the dining board, overturning the glazed pitcher, drowning the pies in ale. I know not if I spoke nor if Maude spoke nor if she made any move toward me. I have no recollection of what I said or did. The thing I next recall was standing in the courtyard in front of my master's house, not knowing how I got there, still clutching the roses.

I threw them in the gutter and crushed each one under my foot. A passing woman gasped. I turned on her like a savage animal, baring my teeth. She ducked and backed away; her eyes round with horror. I must have looked a monster. I must have looked insane. My head . . . my head wanted to explode. I held it together between clenched fists. "Why?" I gasped.

A foolish question; I knew so even then. Maude never was nor ever would be mine.

From the Journal of Jonathan Purchell
28 April, Anno Domini 1375

Two names from Simon's ledgers, Petre Rightwys and Walter Bidick: these are the clerks who preceded me.

Already I have questioned the locals about them. Few remember, and none care a whit about what became of them. London is a crowded city, they say. People move from place to place. True enough, but the wardens do keep a record of the citizens who dwell within their wards. I will question them all.

Perhaps it is time I review what I do in Simon's employ. I keep his business accounts by recording bills of lading for the import and export of commodities in which he invests. I calculate taxes owed and taxes paid, write billings and receipts to his creditors and debtors. I am privy to almost all his business affairs, and by my reckoning, Simon Ratiker is a very wealthy man.

It is extraordinary. The man has no craft. He grows no crop, nor wool, nor employs weavers of cloth, yet he makes profit in all these things and more through buying one commodity and trading it for another.

He rarely leaves his house. Attends no church. Keeps no servants. Meals he has delivered hot from the tavern across the street. He hires a crone to tidy his rooms. This I know only because once each week she climbs too early into the attic and stumbles over my three-legged stool. He keeps his own personal accounts, leaving me to wonder how he spends his money, which most certainly is not in rewarding his clerk although he has the cheek to say he pays me well.

In truth, the man's wealth does not surprise me. I do envy, but do not doubt his business acumen, though how he came by it remains a mystery. Simon is not a man of great learning. He writes poorly and reads haltingly, mouthing the words. But I can testify that he reads a ledger with wicked accuracy.

Now he grows old. He hires a clerk to spare himself labor, but pays ill, and an ill-paid clerk will soon give notice if given the chance. No mystery there. How many clerks over . . . what? Ten years? Twenty? A fair number I'll venture. Still, I become ever more curious about those men who have gone to Ratiker, left, and never returned.

Where did they go?

In veritate scribo,
Johannes P.

Simon describes his encounter with a street raker

Damn me for my weakness, my cowardice, my stubborn refusal to accept the truth. Maude did not love me! Not as I loved her. I knew that, but I would not accept it. I could not. I would not abandon all my hopes.

Like thunder and lightning, the throbbing pain continued to storm in my head as I wandered the streets beyond my ward. At last, leaving my carcass bag outside, I entered a tavern unfamiliar to me. I must have looked suspect for the ale-wench refused to serve me until she saw my coin. Surprised she was when I reached into my boot and drew out a full-round shilling. She accepted my reckoning and drew away, her eyes still wide with surprise. While waiting her return, I listened to the gossip flowing around me: mostly about the plague, from whence it came, who and how many dead, and how to escape it. Everywhere, talk only of plague. "A pox on the plague!" I cried aloud. No one paid me heed.

I retreated to the voices arguing within my head. It was an old argument, well rehearsed, memorized. Back and forth it went, "Thou, Rat Taker, who would love thee? It is only a charity that Maude feels for you, a kindness she would afford any stray who begs at her door." Thoughts such as these vied with others as equally discomforting: "If you truly love her, it is her happiness that you must wish for. She will value you all the more for it. And is not a valued friendship more worthy, more to be desired than fickle love?"

At times the voice of Hope would intervene: "You cannot know what she feels for Amaury. He may love her, but Maude does not believe in love. You cannot say that his is a love returned." I would cling to this thought like a drowning man until another wave of crushing certainty overwhelmed me.

The truth, I now suspect, was somewhere else entirely, but I could not consider it then: my own measure of self-worth, small as it was, obscured a more possible truth that would have been even harder to accept.

Our vanity does often shield us from sterner self-judgments, does it not? Although I thought myself lowly as dung, I still believed that Maude did give countenance to my existence, and that, if only for charity's sake, I did occupy her thoughts. It never occurred to me that she was indifferent. Thus are we bound to our fruitless hopes, and willingly so, for who among us can withstand the thought of being outside the mind and heart of the one person we love.

* * *

To my surprise, old tears, long unspent, rose up from deep within me. I did not care that people saw and thought me drunk. I did not care. Other patrons removed themselves from my company so that I was left entirely alone, which suited me.

I at last slumped over my ale-cup wanting only to sleep. Had I a desire for anything at that moment, it was to take to my bed for an extended slumber, after which to arise and leave London forever.

I would, perhaps, join the King's legions to fight in France, possibly to die in a bloody field, to be buried with my unlucky past — gone from the memory of man. Or perhaps I would return to Cornwall, and after being beaten senseless for running away, go down into the mine pits that would kill me no less certainly than the King's war. That prospect seemed both better and worse than becoming a soldier. Better because I would be home free to breathe the clean air of Cornwall, worse because I would be home, no less a slave to the mines than I was to my London master. Soldier or miner? The more I thought on these options, the less they appealed, so that in the end I felt no ambition to pursue either.

Woozy with ale, I had just laid my head on the table, welcoming oblivion, when a breath, heavy with rank meat and sour ale, stirred against my neck.

"Full heavy grows our bag of woes until it feels like riches," whispered a drunken voice. Then it pulled back and said, lightly, "I will match my woes against yours, Goodson, if you but share your ale."

I turned my head away. "Go to the Devil."

"Misery does love company, my friend."

"Aye, but you stink."

"As do you."

I glanced then at the man sitting beside me. "True, but I bear it through familiarity. Your stink is passing strange."

He nodded drunkenly as he emptied the last of my ale into his cup and signaled the serving wench for more.

Through blurry eyes, I at last recognized Hodge, the street raker from my own ward. I groaned. "Hodge, damn you. Am I then so close to home?"

"You want not to be?" he asked with indifference.

"Home is a foreign place."

"And London is a bung hole! Let us quit this city. Where shall we go?"

I looked at him stupidly. "There is nowhere."

"Ah! But here there is ale! So here is where I shall drink and die!" He sloshed his cup in a drunken toast and farted hugely before he drank. The serving wench arrived with more ale. Hodge poured for us both.

I was after all glad to have someone to talk

to, and Hodge was a merry fellow in spite of his rude farts. I knew little about him beyond what I saw: a man not old, not young, paunch bellied, bow-legged, eyes like prunes, a nose not centered and hair thick and black as stringy tar. On that day, his filthy tunic was crusty with dried blood from the horse he had earlier dismembered. He was a man born to his trade yet he lived above it with a whistle and a jest.

"So tell me, Goodson," he said, bending into my face, "what has brought you so low?"

"Sweet fellow, my day be as foul as your breath," I replied, drawing away. "And how is it you ask what brings me low? We are on a level, are we not? Answer for yourself and you shall have my answer. I am a rat taker."

"That makes you weep? Christ's foot! What would London be without street rakers and rat takers?"

"London still, but I would be a man."

"Faith, Simon! You are a whoreson and nothing better. Shame on you for insulting good ale with your sorrows!"

I took a deep swallow from my full cup letting the taste linger on my tongue. "It's not that good. So," I asked, "What did you do with the dead horse?"

"Oh, did you see that? Jésu, what a filthy job! It makes me thirsty all over again just to think about it." He poured more ale, drank lustily, and slammed his cup on the table so hard it shattered.

"But what did you do with it?"

"Why? Do you want it? It is a very dead horse."

The serving wench brought a fresh cup and mopped the table, while I told Hodge about my horsehide nellies. Hodge stared openmouthed at my vest, picking at it and seeing wealth unbounded. "The devil, you say. Horsehide repels fleas? How did I not know this? This calls for a new fashion in horsehide. Horsehide caps, horsehide shoes, a whole wardrobe of horsehide! Every whoreson and his bride will want it!"

"Aye, and horsemeat is passably tasty," said I, warming to the subject. "The blood does enrich the soil, and even the contents of the bladder, be it full, is worth a few farthings. A valuable thing is a dead horse."

"More valuable dead than alive," he agreed. "I'm beginning to feel somewhat richer."

"How often do they die in the street?"

"Not often enough."

I laughed aloud, a drunken guffaw that made heads turn even in that noisy room. Though I knew him not well, at that moment it did seem that Hodge was my best friend in the world.

We talked at length of horsehide fortunes and how to get them. I was too drunk to remember even one of our clever designs, but I'm sure they were inventive if not wholly practical. It was a careless afternoon, and for an hour or so I forgot my woes.

When daylight began to wane, I bestirred myself, remembering I had one unfinished task to complete: the crack in the church foundation. I had promised myself I would do that one thing before I went to bed. Hodge helped me to my feet as I helped him to his, then leaning into each other we left the tavern.

My friend Hodge, aye, now do I call him friend. Yet, many months it was before I realized he was no longer there. Seeing him gone, I held a hope that he had indeed made his fortune in horsehide and traveled to another place, but my heart knew otherwise. I felt sorry that we had not said a proper farewell. Though I can't say I grieved overly, for our acquaintanceship was distant and impersonal except for that one afternoon when drink made us cronies.

From the Journal of Jonathan Purchell
30 July, Anno Domini 1375

Something is queerly amiss with Master Ratiker. He is vastly changed so that I wonder for his health.

It has been a month over since his last dictation. Thrice during this time he has come to my attic room as if to resume his narrative. Instead, he sits and stares into space with troubled eyes, uttering nary a word. He cannot seem to find his direction. I read back to him what has so far been written. He listens as if it were someone else's story. He then sighs and leaves me.

What is more, he increasingly leaves the managing of his business to me, as if he is losing all interest in commerce. I have taken to signing his name to documents that need timely attention. He cares not. In fact, he seems inclined to give me complete license in this regard.

But he watches. I feel his eyes following me, and when I catch him out, his eyes do not waver but continue to look into mine without expression so that I shiver and must turn away. Sometimes methinks he is taking my measure for some weighty enterprise as yet unrevealed to me, but then I don't know and fall into thinking there is a darker purpose.

So unsettling is the atmosphere, I have thought to leave, simply pack up my few possessions and leave. Then I am reminded of the clerks who came before, their undiscovered fate, and of my own avowed purpose to uncover the secrets buried in this house. Besides, where would I go? How would I live? So here I remain, but for how much longer I cannot say.

In veritate scribo,
Johannes P.

From the Journal of Jonathan Purchell
15 August, Anno Domini 1375

A full two weeks have passed and still no more dictation from Master Ratiker.

He broods and mutters to himself. He eats little, often returning his tray without tasting the food. Widow Truwet from the tavern across the street is beside herself thinking that he has ceased to enjoy her cooking. I assured her that the food is without fault, having on occasion helped myself to the cold victuals before she came to collect the tray.

Widow Truwet, a robust woman whose excellent cooking keeps her late husband's tavern in good custom, has proved to be an unexpected source of information. Some days ago, she revealed to me that Ratiker has suffered melancholy in the past, but none so deep that he has failed to eat. She spoke in a whisper under the solar stairs, "You won't be leaving, now will you?" Before I could answer, she added with certainty, "You will. They all do." I inquired as to her meaning, and she revealed that whenever the master falls into one of his black humours, his clerk leaves. Apparently this has happened so often she wonders that Ratiker's business hasn't fallen into ruin. She went on to say that she hoped I would not abandon my master as have the others because "Master Ratiker is a sad, lonely man who has no friends, and a steadfast clerk would be a boon in his old age," at least in her humble opinion. Then, with a high blush, she left hurriedly with her tray, leaving me to believe the poor woman has feelings for old Simon.

I confess with some chagrin that I never thought to question the widow about Simon's former clerks, an oversight born of my prejudices against the other gender. It is a failing of all men, I trow, but I should have remembered that it is women who know the comings and goings, births, deaths and vices of all the neighbors. Gossip is their very breath. Men have no patience for such things; they being more interested in market values, taxes, tithes and like matters of a higher nature.

Seizing an opportunity to further my investigation, I visited the widow's tavern the next evening. Entering by the kitchen door, I found the good woman shelling peas by lamplight. Two sculleries cleaned up after the day's custom, filling the space with much clatter and bang. The next day's bread baked in stone ovens outside the yard door; its yeasty aroma wafted into the room.

Widow Truwet greeted me warmly. Before I could tell her my purpose for being there, she sat me down at her worktable and offered a cold chop and ale. I accepted and ate greedily, but wasted no time getting to the point. "Tell me," I said. "What know you about Master Simon's former clerks?"

"Very little," she replied readily. "They all be men like you: young, schooled, quiet and into themselves, although the last one, young Bidick, was quite friendly. He courted Mistress Lucy and it seemed the two were a match then he left without a word. Near broke the poor girl's heart."

"Mistress Lucy?"

"One of the serving maids. You know her. Tall and lean."

"Ah!" I did know her: A pale lass with the devil's mark: a slight harelip. She was not pretty, but had a pleasant nature. A simple maid was my impression. "Have you any thoughts about why he disappeared?"

She looked up from her copper bowl and said thoughtfully, "I suppose that is the word, "disappeared," but it does have a ominous sound, does it not? I think he just left. Returned home, I should imagine."

"Home where?"

She shrugged and picked up another peapod. "Lucy might know."

Yes. I would ask Lucy. "But why?" I pressed. "If he and Lucy were betrothed . . ."

"But they were not betrothed, not yet. It was just a feeling that Lucy had, poor lass. She hasn't many suitors and no one to arrange a future for her. No dowry." She gave me a sharp look. "And it's not what you are thinking. Lucy is a good girl. It was none of that sort of thing."

She had read my mind. I smiled in apology, though it was a reasonable assumption. I knew the size of a clerk's wage. Not enough to support a family. Still, if he loved her . . .?

"Nay," she continued. "It wasn't that. But, in truth, there was something odd about him toward the last. Even Lucy said."

I waited, fearing to speak lest the eagerness in my voice stir her curiosity beyond a point I was prepared to satisfy. The sculleries had finished the washing up and were gone. It was only the good widow and myself sitting at the sturdy table with the lamplight dancing off the curve of the copper bowl. The staccato of peas being popped from their pod made a hollow tune, a comfortable sound inviting childhood memories, while the smell of bread just drawn from the oven made me salivate. Mistress Truwet cut me a thick trencher, slathered it with congealed pork drippings and served it to me.

"Master Simon had gone melancholy and took to his bed," she continued. "The lad was doing the work of two, it seemed, without extra wage, but that did not distress him. He was, like you, an able clerk, up to his duties in all ways. Yet he acted as if . . . as if something troubled him, but he did not say, did he." She covered her bowl of peas with a muslin cloth and set it aside.

"Troubled," I repeated. "Do you mean frightened?"

"Frightened? Of what? No, not frightened. Such an idea! Why would you think that?"

Because I am frightened, or nearly so, I thought to myself, but did not say to her.

"Whatever his reason," she said sourly, "I think it is well gone and good riddance to any man who would leave a master without notice, not to mention a sweet maid to whom he had given hopes. Young lads with learning do get above themselves, I say. Think the world dances only to their tune." She concluded this denunciation, and, in effect, our conversation with a pointed look. "But maybe not all of them," she added, as if for the time being to exclude me from this judgment.

This morning I spoke to Lucy. The tavern was lively with customers, giving her little time to talk. I was brief. "Lucy, I need to find Walter Bidick to pay him back wages." It was a lie, but one that gave good excuse for my interest in her former suitor.

"Well, I should hope so," she lisped. Her face went slack with private grief, and I feared she would start crying. "He fairly wore himself out working for that horrible old stott."

"Do you know where he went, Lucy?"

"Home, I expect," she answered. Her disfigured lip began to twitch. I would soon lose her to tears.

"And where is that, Lucy?"

"Devon, he once told me. Then another time he said Oxford,

but that is where he went to university, so I expect Devon it is."

"And you never heard from him? Not even a note?"

Her eyes flashed angrily as she quickly cleared the remains of my meal. "And what is that to you?" Tears welled in her eyes. She swiped them away.

"I am sorry," I began. "I just hoped . . ." but it was no good. She left before I had time to ask further questions. I left my reckoning on the table and took myself hence having learned very little.

So where did he go, this Walter Bidick, without a note or a word? Simon had said that he left to attend to family business, but what nature of business that he did not, or could not, mention it to Lucy? Something sudden, unexpected and so dire that it warranted immediate action, was that it? Yet strange, is it not, that he has not been seen or heard from since?

Though it is little enough on which to pin my hopes, I do have one course to follow. I will send an agent to Devon — and to Oxford if necessary. It will cost me the price of new leather boots and pair of hose, a sum I can ill afford, but I will pay it. I will borrow from Simon's cash box if I must, so determined am I to see this through. My need to know Bidick's fate has become urgent.

In veritate scribo,
Johannes P.

From the Journal of Jonathan Purchell
9 September, Anno Domini 1375

Ratiker has abandoned all interest in his business, leaving me in full charge.

D ays pass during which we do not speak. Then, without ceremony, he will invite conversation, and I discover myself engaged in some unlikely discourse completely unrelated to business or even to that Fateful Day with which he seems morbidly obsessed.

He has a vigorous intellect, I have observed. A passing thought will engage his interest and become a subject of intense scrutiny. His preferred manner of argument is analogy, seeking truths within like patterns found in nature, although logic is not beyond his ken. He has, however, no patience with the mode of logical discourse, dismissing entirely the whereases and therefores that bring order to an argument. He tells me a Dominican monk once tutored him in Scholastic discourse. Simon smiles at the memory, saying that the monk had rejoiced in his babe-like ignorance and could not resist trying to mold his mind. The mold did not set, I fear. Simon's arguments are mostly ill-construed fragments from schoolboy lessons, impossible to follow.

"Clerk," he says to me one day, "what think you of that spider?"

I glanced up from the ledger in which I was writing and followed his gaze to a small black spider dangling beneath the lip of my candlestick. "It is spinning a web."

"Yes, 'tis so, but why?"

"To catch flies, perhaps?"

"Yes, but why spin a web? Flies do not spin to catch their meat. Nor do beetles, nor foxes, nor man."

I put down my quill and waited, knowing that the obvious answer to his question was not the one he sought.

Simon bent into a closer look. "See you how it exudes filament, how it traces the pattern of a web across the empty, unpatterned space?" He glanced up at me, his eyes round and darkly dangerous. "God gave this creature an advantage, Clerk, an advantage singular in all creation. I ask you why?"

He waited for me. When I failed to respond, he answered himself, "Methinks the answer lies in the spider's purpose."

"To catch flies?"

He shook his head. "That is a necessity, not a purpose. But think, now. Is not every being in creation a fragment of God's truth? And because His truth is indivisible, does not each fragment contain the whole of it?"

"So? This is a paradox no man can fathom," I mumbled.

"Yes, a paradox. And how is that paradox woven into the spider's web? For it is the web itself, I now think, that defines the spider's purpose. It reveals to us the whole of God's truth. We speak of the web of truth, do we not?"

"Aye, and the web of deceit also."

He cocked his head and grinned wolfishly. "Exactly!"

And so on. These mock dialogues do vex me, verily.

I now have full run of the house, no room is closed to me, but the atmosphere is too oppressive. I do my work and escape as soon as I am able, either to the tavern or to the enclosure behind the house. I cannot call it a garden for the area is much overgrown; yet the air is cool off the river and the grassy scrub is dotted with purple bluets and yellow cinquefoils, hangers-on from days of former glory, so that my interludes there make a pleasant change. I retreat now to this patch of earth for a part of each afternoon. It revives my spirits.

It is the same yard, I now realize. Recognition came to me on Wednesday last. It is the same garden behind the same house in which Simon lived with his master. Strange that I did not suspect it sooner and more strange that it affected me so violently when I did, as if it were unnatural that the old man should be living here still. I simply never once considered it.

I was walking through high grass following a nearly invisible path, when my eyes fell on a hedge trimmed to the ground, now no more than unruly branches springing from old roots, irrepressible as nature is when left to itself. I must have noticed the hedge before, the yard is not that big, but this time I saw it and I knew.

Beyond the ragged barrier of branches, the earth forms a low rise rounded at the top, not unlike a new grave. Perhaps that is what made me recoil. It is the old lime pit, long filled in and overgrown with spindly scrub. I stepped on it and felt it solid beneath my feet. The earth, to all appearances, has not been disturbed for years, but it is what it is nonetheless and I do not like it.

The shed that had stood against the wall is gone. A few sticks and a rag, half-consumed by worms, is all that remain. I poked about but could find no clue as to when the shed was torn down except for my own feeling that it was long ago.

While I was examining the site, a prickling touched my skin. Hairs rose on my neck. I turned abruptly and looked at the house. Simon stood at the solar window, watching. We stared at each other for a full while then he backed away into the shadow of the room never taking his eyes from me. For the briefest moment, I felt afraid, then a breeze came over the wall reminding me that I was in London and that the house was just a house after all. The garden was just a garden gone woeful from neglect, and the pit was only a memory, a pit no more. I kicked a stone free of the dry earth. It flew into the wall and bounced back, landing near my shoe like a dog returning to play. I kicked it again and went back to work.

That evening, Simon came to the attic and resumed his dictation.

In veritate scribo,
Johannes P.

Simon's discourse approaches the truth he dreads

I come now to the most difficult part of my tale. I shrink from it and yet am bound to continue. My memory desires to shape the events of that August day into a final truth so that I may judge my own actions in their entirety. It is the truth I seek, and I shall know peace only when I find it. Yet it is the truth I fear, for truth is a multi-bodied beast, so that one must entertain all its diversities and contradictions until the whole of it is at last revealed. Only then may the truth be fairly judged. I approach this beast with caution, knowing that any one of its parts may devour me before I have accomplished my purpose. Aye, that could happen. So I continue my quest, both in hope and in trepidation.

It was late afternoon when I returned to the house that day. Maude was out. My master, who spent each afternoon at Customs Hall, had not returned, most likely taking his evening repast at a friend's table or at a tavern. My master enjoyed a game of chess in the evening and would often play until curfew with some like-minded companion. I didn't mind that no person greeted me. The house was welcoming enough, inviting me to bed where I might sleep off the excess of drink and ease my heartache in dream. But I, with the mulishness of a drunk, went purposefully about my last task of the day, to mortar the crack in the church's foundation, confident that my addled wits would allow it.

I entered the kitchen, noting as I passed through to the yard door that Maude was not there and the kitchen tidy. Platters, tray and pitcher had been washed and put on the shelf. My master's walking stick lay on the sideboard, next to a cleaning agent. Maude had been polishing the silver handle. I wondered where she had gone and when she would return, but mentally sidestepped all thoughts of our next meeting, leaving that inevitable encounter to unfold as it would. Before stepping through the door, I glanced toward the window where the solitary rose still stood, a black silhouette within a square of dying light. The door quietly shut behind me.

I stood for a moment on the stoop, breathing deeply to clear my lungs of tavern air as I watched the sun slip behind the rooftops.

To this day, any warm August evening brings with it the memory of that one evening, and even more sharply that singular moment when I stepped into the yard. The air had grown still, not a breeze stirring. Birdcalls came from all around, but not a bird could be seen. I sensed the street mongers had dispersed with the last peal of vesper bells, their shadows trailing behind or stretching before like misshapen cats. For a long moment I stood listening for something yet out of tune with the dwindling day, but all was soft and smooth and harmonious. All was lullaby. And waiting.

How can I describe the waiting? Even without the constant mentioning in every church and tavern, one could not for a moment forget the fearful scourge raking across the land. Appalling news of its progress, each report more urgent than the last, arrived every day, slipping through the warden's barricades with ease, infecting every household like a disease itself. The fearful certainty that Londoners would not be spared this most awful of visitations loomed over everything, clouding every tenuous hope with dire prediction. Even Father Liam's worthy prayers could not lessen the magnitude of our fear. We lived in apprehension. Prayer offered no solace and faith no sureties.

Perhaps 'tis but a trick of memory, but I think I knew then, on that fair August evening, that the pestilence was no longer approaching but had arrived. Twice since have I witnessed its coming and have surmised that this Great Death rides in on little things: a fallen feather, a sprinkle of spice, a rat's whisker. It well could be that even then I recognized its harbingers in the tiny corpses lying twisted in the streets and cellars of the ward. I must have done so because, for the second time that day, I was overcome with grief, not for myself, but for my city.

The moment passed, and I, stiffening my resolve, addressed my task with drunken determination. I gathered from my shed the ingredients for making mortar: a bag of quicklime, a bag of sand, a pail of water and a paddle for mixing. With my unwieldy burden I returned to the house and opened the cellar door. Halfway down my tottering descent into the darkness, I stopped and cursed my stupidity. I had forgotten to bring a lamp.

I then remembered that a lamp and flint box sat on a shelf near the bottom of the cellar stair, so I continued down. Undeterred by the enveloping dark and the unevenness of the old granite steps, I proceeded downward, twice missing my footing but recovering in time to avoid injury. The moment I stepped onto the cellar floor, I set down my burden and reached for the oil lamp. It was not there.

As I have mentioned, I was familiar with all the cellars within my ward, but none so much as my master's. Though the plan of it was complex, with several small rooms radiating off the large central chamber, it was not difficult, once my eyes became accustomed to the dark, to discern the faint outlines of portals leading to the other rooms. In one of these side rooms was a door that opened onto the passage leading to St. Michael Paternoster's foundation. That is where I wished to go, but I could not proceed into the passage without a lamp. I began a search, although how the lamp could be anywhere but on the shelf was a most troubling mystery to my muddled head.

My master was an orderly man. For him, each thing in life had its place. This quirk of his nature extended from the smallest detail of his daily affairs to the contents of his cellar, which was a marvel of organization. One of the rooms contained business records neatly stacked in labeled boxes lined side by side upon sturdy shelves. Two rooms served as a kind of warehouse for wine and sample commodities in which he traded. There, too, the kegs, boxes and bales sat side by side on raised wooden pallets. One wall of the central chamber had been converted into a storehouse for dry goods and food preserves, each item occupying a designated shelf. Once you knew the arrangement of the shelves, you could find what you needed in total darkness because each item was exactly where it was supposed to be. Maude kept the cellar free of webs and insects. My job, of course, was to eliminate the rodents. One could have lived comfortably within that underground chamber; so tidy it was, so like my master.

After searching the central chamber high and low, I found no lamp, no candle, nothing to light my way. Had my wits been clearer, I would have left my task for another day, but I was drunk and hell-bent to complete my charge. Father Liam expected me to seal the crack in the church's old foundation, and seal the crack, I would!

I stood in the darkness trying to deal with my predicament. The logical course, which was to go back to the kitchen and get a lamp, seemed inordinately complex. I believe I finally reached the decision to sit down on the floor and wait for the lamp to reveal itself. That's when I heard the voices.

The sound came not from the yard, as one would expect, but from somewhere underground. I heard the voices again, followed by a playful bark. Even in my drunken confusion, I knew it was Pye. I followed the sounds through a door into a side chamber. The room was empty save for a few slivers of light escaping through cracks in the door opposite: the door that opened into the underground passage.

I understood in an instant the implication of my discovery, and was shocked sober. Aye, I had found at last the missing lamp. It was there just beyond the passage door in a place where I no longer wanted to go.

Pye whimpered behind the door and scratched at the hard earth. I drew back just as Amaury spoke, "Away, Pye. Get away from there." Then to Maude, "She smells a rat."

I waited. When it seemed that Pye was calmed, I returned to the door and put my eye to one of the wider cracks giving a fairly clear view of the room beyond. Though I feared what I would see, I was unable not to look. I had to know everything.

They sat together on a bedrobe, their backs against the earthen wall. Pye sat quivering next to her master, staring at the door, but she remained blessedly silent. The lamp was set apart, near the edge of the robe, but not so far that I couldn't see all I needed. Maude had curled herself into Amaury's arms, her gown and fresh apron spread modestly around her legs and feet. I watched her brush the front of Amaury's jacket with gentle fingers as he whispered into her hair. She looked up at him with a dazzling smile that set her eyes aglow. I watched Amaury kiss her forehead, her temple, her brow then gaze into her eyes now languid with love. Slowly he traced with his fingertip the curve of her cheek, her mouth. I watched Maude kiss his finger as he touched the scar on her lip, the tiny scar I loved so much.

I moaned inwardly. Never had she abided with me in such a way. Never. I was undone.

From the Journal of Jonathan Purchell
15 September, Anno Domini 1375

There can no longer be any doubt. Simon is seriously unbalanced.

He came early this evening and began to rant about the nature of truth, the truth within truth, all manner of truth including God's, as he paced the narrow corridor outside my room. I could not untangle a word of his meaning. I did try to listen with sympathy, knowing his distress was genuine, but was at a loss.

Hoping to ease his agitation, I offered to beckon a street lad to run to the tavern for a calming brew. Simon declined, waving the suggestion aside as he would an annoying servant. When I attempted to prod his memory with gentle interrogation, he would look at me sidelong and say, "In good time," or something equally cryptic, so that I was at a loss to know his direction, while he, in some way sly and secret, appeared always to know his exact heading.

The hour was late, but Simon was far from sleep, as was I. It was a night for revelations, and we were both ready for it, but something was holding Simon back. Like a dog on a short leash, he strained against a stronger force that would not let him go forward.

"Simon," I said, "What of your master? You have never told me his name."

"He has little part in this," he answered brusquely.

"But I would know for myself," I persisted, hoping to find a back-end route into his story. "Did he apprentice you in his trade? Did he bequeath you his enterprises along with this house?"

To my relief, Simon took no offense at my impudent inquiry, but drew one long breath and settled into quietude.

"I must sit," he said.

"Sit," I urged, moving aside the folded robe at the foot of the cot.

He eased himself down onto the narrow mattress and sat quietly a moment more while I waited. When he spoke, I simply listened without attempting to write.

"In the end, my master neither apprenticed nor bequeathed me, and I am certain he had no intention to do either. He was not a generous man. Even if he had, and I had shown an aptitude for commerce, there was no time to teach me once the pestilence arrived."

Again, a long pause during which Simon sat chair-like, both hands on his knees, his eyes screwed shut against the dim light of my lamp. His face, half in shadow, resembled a grotesque mask, the false face of a jester or fool. When his voice came again, it was barely a whisper. "It is hard to speak of those days."

He worked his jaw, grinding his teeth while tears gathered in his eyes. I was moved by his sorrow and was amazed. That an old sorrow could still cut so deep, a old, old sorrow yet still so fresh. I myself was a child who lived during the second coming of plague 1n 1361 and those are cruel days to remember. Two in ten citizens died that year, among them my own mother, father, and two sisters. When, during our first meeting, I did speak of this to Simon, I sensed a softening in his manner, as if he truly felt my loss. Now as I watched slow tears coursing down his cheeks, I felt most deeply the sorrow in us both.

"The plague took him, then?" I prompted.

Simon began to tremble violently. I unfolded my bedrobe and draped it across his shoulders. He seemed not to notice. His teeth chattered so hard, he could not speak. I waited. When the seizure passed, Simon fell back upon the bed and stared at the slanted ceiling. The cap he always wore fell off his head and lay apart.

"Aye," he said at last. "If I read the signs aright, it was the plague that took him. At the time I could only guess, for a strange sickness also fell upon me and took me to the very doors of hell. In my absence, death came for my master and took his soul without God's final forgivness.

"It is hard to speak of those days," he repeated, pressing the sides of his head between clenched fists. "Events tangle in my mind so that I cannot separate one horror from another — events too terrible to speak aloud, and yet I must speak them. I must untangle the truth that lies within or be forever confounded."

Simon rose from the bed, trailing the robe behind him. He again paced the corridor outside my room as his words began to spew forth. I believe he forgot that I was there. I grabbed up a new quill and began to write.

In veritate scribo,
Johannes P.

In which Simon tells of the plague and of his deepest sorrow

Maude and Amaury were lovers. I now knew the certainty of it and realized that even in my deepest despair, I had harbored a hope that she was, in truth, my Maude and only mine. Now I could see her with him, see her loving him as she had never loved me. I watched as they touched, teased, and slipped into intimate pleasures while whispering words of desire. How often had they been together, I wondered? How often had she greeted me with smiling lips still warm from Amaury's kiss? How often had she been lost in his embrace while I was away yet holding her in my heart? Whether once or a hundred times it did not matter. She loved Amaury. She loved him. The misery of this knowledge drove me to my knees.

I wanted to hurt them. Hateful words not uttered hammered against my heart. Let them die together!

Suddenly, like a rapier's stab, my headache pierced my brain. I must have swooned, for the next I knew I lay at the foot of the cellar stairs, my face in a puddle of sour bile. I vomited again when I tried to stand, and again as I dragged myself up the granite steps into the night. The pounding, pounding in my head staggered my steps, beat me down to the ground, forcing me to crawl forward to make progress until I at last made it to my room and fell onto my bed.

An icy pain, so acute I could not lay a-straight, invaded my every extremity. I tossed and moaned in torment without a moment's relief. Then came the fever, exciting my brain with visions of such a hellish nature I believed myself dead and among the damned. I would not accept my fate, unconscious though I was; and while my body tossed on the bed, my soul wrestled with demons. Days and nights uncounted, for I knew not one from the other, slipped away while I struggled up from hell. I cried for help, but no one came.

Was it the pestilence or brain fever? I do not know, only that delirium took me entirely and played hellish tricks with my mind. When at last the fever abated and my senses revived, I crawled out of my bed as weak and befouled as a babe, but that mattered naught to me. I cared only to find some breathing being to be assured that I was still among the living. What I found was my master dead in his bed and Maude missing.

London, I soon discovered, had changed while I was ill. The plague was upon us. Streets were deserted of people. The gutters ran foul with filth unattended. Seeing how the dead were left on door fronts, I mustered strength enough to drag my master's body from his bed and into the street where I left it rolled in a sheet. The cart came and took it away. Later I learned that the body was carried to Smithfield where hundreds were buried together in common graves. Day after day I watched the same cart carry away my neighbors. Some faces were recognizable, others so bloated and discolored as to be beyond recognition. Church bells tolled continuously until one day all the bells ceased and a terrible silence descended over the city, a silence even more terrible for the one cry that continued in the streets.

"Bring out your dead!"

When a measure of my strength returned, I carried my master's bed, board by board, out of the house, tossed it into the lime pit, and set it aflame. While it burned, I listened in vain for some familiar sound: Pye barking at crows, maid Alyce stepping through her master's gate, street mongers crying their wares, Maude calling from the kitchen door. No sound satisfied. There came only the crackling heat from within the burning pit and a cry in the street calling for the dead.

I returned to the house, closed the door, and there I vowed to stay until the pestilence ran its course. Food enough in the cellar sustained my body, though just barely.

To occupy my mind, to keep from going mad,

I turned to my master's account books and documents of trade. The names of his merchant suppliers were all foreign to me. I could read no words beyond corn, wine, and wool, and had to guess at the rest, but being modestly educated in numbers, the ledgers eventually became clearer to me. I first noticed how the numbers increased in some columns, decreased in others to finally balance out over a period of weeks. I discovered I had a knack for numbers and spent hours each day reading the ledgers. I slowly comprehended the breadth of my master's enterprises and was amazed.

Father Liam visited me as a charity, bringing food and news of the parish. At first he came infrequently and stayed briefly, only long enough to recite the names of those who had died and those who had left the ward. I remember him telling me that the vintner's house next door stood empty. He could not account for the whereabouts of the vintner and his family. Of the apprentice, he had no news. Later he visited more often and stayed longer. The two of us would sit for hours by the great hearth in which a fire always burned to hinder a chance of contagion. He began to teach me how to read.

The only reading material in the house other than my master's ledgers was The Book of Psalms, so that is what we used. Father Liam preferred the psalms that prophesied Christ, and most especially Psalm 22, "My God, My God, why hast thou forsaken me?" I can recite that psalm fully to this day.

Before leaving, Father Liam would give me a single verse to study, charging me to write all the words I could read in one list and all the rest in a second list. On his next visit he would teach me the letters and sounds and sense of the words I did not know. Before long, the first list began to grow longer than the second. I made good progress.

Often when Father Liam read a verse aloud the meaning remained clouded, and I would pause in my struggle with the letters to ask for clarification. Then would we talk long on some point of faith. I was full of questions.

"The Psalmist continually entreats God not to abandon him," I once remarked, "and it does seem that God has abandoned us all, does it not?" It was the sound of the death cart just below my window that had prompted my question.

Father Liam went to the window and said prayers over the bodies as they rolled past before he rejoined me by the fire.

"No, Simon, He has not abandoned us," he replied without expression.

I saw for the first time how very tired he was. I later learned that he was one of the few priests who continued to administer the last rites and to comfort plague victims both living and dying.

"We are His children," he said as if by rote, "and He loves us, for God is Love and cannot do otherwise. Never forget that, Simon. He cannot do otherwise."

He paused to give the fire logs a fierce prod. The fire spat and sent sparks onto the hearth-stones. "His one purpose is to bring all his children into His love. But we resist, don't we? Through our freedom of will, which He granted so we may love him freely, we resist. We disobey. We are wayward children, verily, who will not accept the conditions of His love for fear of losing all else."

His voice was strained and I realized with a surprise of satisfaction that Father Liam was angry with God. A door sprung open within me, releasing emotions I had locked away, believing them shameful. It felt good, like a breath of cold air after an arduous climb. "That is how He made us," I said with some bitterness.

"Possibly. God's ways are mysterious. We cannot know what is in the mind of God. But this I do believe, in spite of everything, He will never abandon us."

After that, nothing was beyond the bounds of our discussions: doubt, speculation, even the heresies that drew folk away from the True Faith.

I asked him one evening, "If as you say, Father, we are redeemed through our sufferings, why did Christ die for our sins?"

He shook his head. "Man cannot redeem himself. But you are correct in part, Man must redeem himself"

He saw the question in my eyes and continued, "So God became Man and died for men's sins. That is how much He loves us, Simon. He never has nor ever will abandon us."

I never fully understood this mystery and, in truth, never did fully believe, but I did believe in Father Liam and so remembered his words in faith.

I came to depend on the good Father's visits and grew fretful when he stayed too long away. Then came a period in which he did not come. I waited by the window willing him to come, but he never did. It was the deacon who brought the news that Father Liam had died.

From autumn to autumn and on into the following spring, the siege continued. The summer of 1349 was the worst, with near to three hundred citizens dying each day. But we were all dead by then, if not in body, then in spirit, for there was too much grief for too few living hearts to bear.

Then, one cold morning in early spring, the church bells broke their long silence and pealed loudly throughout the city. I went uncloaked into the street. Others joined me. No joy marked our meeting, only relief and some wonderment that we had somehow survived. I cannot recall anyone speaking a word.

Gradually, citizens returned to the business of living, though disconnected from each other like broken threads in a rotted rag. Yet, as all men know, life goes on. The city began to mend itself, shakily at first then growing stronger until some semblance of its former vigor was restored.

Nonetheless, a different world emerged from those dreadful days. Vast vacancies in the city's merchant houses crippled day-to-day enterprise. Every man was left to make his own way, sometimes by taking what others had left behind: houses, shops, fortunes.

My master, having been childless, left no immediate heir. I knew he had brothers somewhere. I waited for them to come with their claim. They never did. After a time, I assumed whoever might have inherited my master's estate was also dead.

My own claim was but a foundling's stipend written into my master's will. After a suitable time, I petitioned the Chancery for the entire estate. My petition was granted. Thus did I seize the opportunity to better my station. I donned my master's coat, though it was an uneasy fit, and stepped into the world of commerce. A priest from Chancery School continued my reading lessons. I hired bright young clerks to manage my master's accounts while I watched and learned. In time, I made my own business alliances in the name of Simon Ratiker. No one questioned my right to do this. No one seemed to care. Anyone who might have protested was gone.

So many were gone, and I grieved for them, yet only one did I truly mourn. I call it mourning, but it was more. My grief for her settled within me like a second soul. I could not shake it. I could not stop wanting the love I had desired of her, the love I had hoped for yet never attained and did grieve the more for never having attained it. Like a father cradling his dying child, I did cling to my love for Maude, knowing that no other love and no other kind of loving could fill the emptiness she had left behind.

From the Journal of Jonathan Purchell
22 September, Anno Domini 1375

Simon's behavior alters more each day.

He prowls the house as one searching for a lost trinket, his manner sometimes furtive, sometimes agitated, but never at peace. It is as if beetles were nibbling at his brain. Perhaps the unknowable truth of Maud's fate, having already consumed his soul, is now devouring his mind. I can almost believe it so.

His last dictation was heart wrenching. I do confess it moved me, yet a mystery goes unsolved: what became of Maude and her lover? Simon never tries to explain it, which I find most curious.

Today my curiosity drove me to the cellar doors. I had little trouble finding them, buried though they were under heaps of dead vegetation. The door hinges are free of rust, leading me to believe the cellar is not so long abandoned as I had imagined. An iron lock holds the doors fast, yet the lock's great size suggests an uncommon key that I have identified as one among others hanging in the kitchen pantry. Tomorrow, if I can slip away unnoticed, I shall make an expedition into those lower regions.

And now there is this. Walter Bidick did not return to Devon, my agent does assure me. A few of the villagers remembered him. One local reported that the man left Devon six years ago to attend university. Two years ago his mother died, the last of the Bidick family it seems. One old gossip recalled a cousin, but it might have been a family friend, who came to care for the ailing mother. She left after the old woman died, went back to her own family somewhere north of the shire. No one in the village has seen Walter Bidick for years. "Went proud," they said. "Too good for the village. Let his mother die without offering so much as a prayer."

Then on to Oxford. The agent found three Bidicks on the rolls at University and a family of Bidicks living nearby, but none who ever heard of Walter Bidick or Simon Ratiker. So the trail grows cold, and I am three shillings poorer without achieving any satisfaction.

In veritate scribo,
Johannes P.

From the Journal of Jonathan Purchell
24 September, Anno Domini, 1375

I have found Walter Bidick, and where before I complained that the search for him did cost me three shillings, I now fear it has cost me my life.

Simon wants me to complete this story. He left a lamp and quill so that I may complete it, but I will not. I am satisfied that there is no escape for me. I have pursued the limited possibilities and am at last satisfied. I will not escape, but will die here upon a bed of bones and leaves of parchment.

I am locked inside a small room within the cellar. On the far wall is a door, unhinged and scarred by flames, that leads to an underground passage. Just beyond the threshold of this door lie the remains of a dog. Farther back lie two human skeletons. The skull of one lies apart, shattered. The other lies wholly connected, yet twisted and charred among the ashes of flesh and cloth. The door opposite this threshold leads to the main chamber through which I came hours ago. Now the door is barred on the outside and quite unyielding. On the floor between the door to the central chamber and the door to the underground passage lies the body of Walter Bidick. I know it is he because his corpse is the least decomposed of the others. I count six in all, some sprinkled with quicklime, some partially buried, all, it appears, were struck down by blows to the head and face. One of the corpses may be the clerk who preceded Bidick, Petre Rightwys, but I have no way to distinguish which one he is. The air reeks with death's corruption.

My first impulse upon stumbling onto this horror was to flee, realizing that I, too, was in danger of my life. But to flee, I could not. My mind was too numb with shock to tell my legs what to do. I had no desire to examine the corpses, their identity being immediately evident to me. My only thought was to leave, and when my senses returned I would have done so, but then I saw the manuscripts. Curiosity drew me further into the room.

The manuscripts stand against the left wall, over twenty by my count, each loosely bound within a fold of heavy cloth. The ones at the bottom of the stack are old, so old the leaves have darkened from too much damp. I lifted a newer one from the top of the stack. The pages were still supple, the ink still black. I scanned the first page and felt the earth fall from under my feet. I picked up another, then another, and another, ever more disbelieving as each time I read the same opening words: *I remember the day the rats began to die.*

Not one of the manuscripts is complete. All of them stop short of revealing the story's tragic ending. Although the manner of writing varies, the story is the same, always the same.

The pages fell from my hand scattering like dead leaves over the bodies at my feet. What aberration of mind, I wondered, would cause a man to repeat and repeat the same tale without variation? His acts of murder were easy to divine. These sorry clerks had grown too curious. Like me, they had learned Simon's secret. But the manuscripts? For certes, in them lay the very definition of Simon's madness, yet its meaning eluded me. For a moment, fear for my own safety paled within the magnitude of this grotesque puzzle.

What happened in this cellar those many years ago? Damn Simon for his silence! He rambles on about the truth that is unknowable until all within it is known. Yet he refuses to make the known knowable. It is as if he himself does not know what happened. But how could he not? He was there!

I heard the door behind me scrape against the floor and wheeled around in time to see Simon peering in at me just before the door shut. His eyes told me I was a dead man.

"Simon," I said with surprising calm. "What is the meaning?

No answer came, but on the floor inside the threshold sat an unlighted lamp, ink, quills, and the latest version of his tale — my own transcription — along with my journal in which I now write and which, most certainly, Simon has read through. He wants me to continue writing. About what? About what is in this room? To what purpose?

"Damn you thrice over, Simon Ratiker!" I railed. "No longer will I accommodate your whims!"

I decided to burn every last page of the manuscript, and was about to do so when something under foot nearly tripped me over. I had in fact disturbed the remains of Walter Bidick, releasing a curiosity that must have been hidden in Bidick's grasp. I reached for it gingerly, found it hard to my touch and, after lifting it up, heavy in my hand.

A close inspection revealed that the object was a knob handle made of silver turned black with age. It had once capped a wooden stick, but the stick had burned away. Only a charred fragment remained within the hollow base of the handle.

I stared long at my find, at the disfigured design etched into the silver, and wondered about its significance. How long had it been here? From whence did it come? Was it Bidick's? I thought not. Did he bring it with him or find it among the horrors of these rooms? The latter seemed most likely. By the light of the lamp, I studied the bits of charred wood within the base of the handle. My eyes went from that to the blackened skeleton in the underground passage. With increasing excitement, I began placing and replacing the silver handle within the context of Simon's story until it at last slipped into its rightful place.

Now I will take up the manuscript and begin to read Simon's narrative from the beginning. Let us see if with this new evidence I can untangle the story's stubborn knot and make it straight.

Some time has passed, I cannot tell how long. The lamp Simon left behind has almost consumed its oil. My candle has burned its length. I will soon be in pitch-blackness. I have time only to write my conclusion: Simon does not know how Maude and Amaury died. He suspects he killed them, but he cannot remember. It is this uncertainty that has driven him mad for his suspicion wants the certainty of truth, yet he fears what the truth may be.

Such a torment would threaten any man's sanity, verily, and I… The lamp sputters. I will wait now in darkness. He will come. My instincts tell me he will come, and I am ready for him, armed with the truth.

In veritate scribo,
Johannes P.

From the Journal of Jonathan Purchell
30 September, Anno Domini 1375

One week it has been since my last entry. I resume my journal free of my prison, but still trembling from the haunting horror of all that transpired in that place of death.

He came, as I felt he would, though much later than I expected. The light of his torch showed through a crack under the doorframe as he approached. He did not enter, but stood just out-side the barred door. He wanted to talk. He had reached that point in his tale where the threads of memory ripped apart. He had to try once again to connect the dangling ends, hoping that, at last, he would know the truth. I was prepared to reveal the truth, but only if I could stay his murderous intent.

"Clerk?" he summoned.

I did not answer.

"Clerk?" he said with a rise in his voice. "Answer me. What think you now?" He waited for my reply. I did not answer.

"You cower?" he said. "You shake in terror, cursing the day you ever heard the name Simon Ratiker."

That last was true enough, and yet I felt strangely exhilarated, more alive than ever I had before. It was a dangerous game we played, Simon and I. There were no rules, but only my wits against a madman's cunning. My chances of winning were slim, but as long as the game continued so did my life.

I waited, waiting to hear him say my name. I wanted the mad man to say my name.

I heard the bar being raised, quietly, slowly, then drop back into place. He had changed his mind. I watched the light under the door waver and retreat until all was blackness again.

He would return. Of that I felt certain.

I waited a long time; time measured only by savage hunger and thirst. I could no longer smell so keenly the air of death that lay all around me, but the taste of it coated my teeth, my tongue, and filled my throat like foul meat I could not swallow. I felt the presence of my dead companions, the weight of their silence crushing me. They were waiting too, waiting to be discovered and avenged. I had failed them. Simon would not return, they told me. Now I must share their fate. The air was heavy with their smug certainty.

I tried to sleep and could not. I listened for a sound: church bells, dog barks, any sound other than an occasional scuffling of rats, which would connect me with the living. Just one sound for comfort's sake, then could I sleep. There was only silence, a primordial silence so profound that it, too, weighted the darkness.

Time did not exist in that darkness, only an immutable Now within nowhere. I could not think. My mind demanded the familiar dimension of time in which to build its edifices. It wanted the scaffold of an idea. It wanted a voice to respond to. My thoughts turned delusional.

"Walter?" I whispered. I awaited an answer in mad expectation,.

"Walter?" I asked again, this time louder. "How did you come to this sorry pass?"

"Answer for yourself," came the reply in a voice too like Simon's, "and you shall have my answer. Are we not on a level, you and I?"

I thought on this reply, unexpected yet so appropriate, and laughed inwardly. Truly, we were brethren, Walter and I, brethren in Simon Ratiker whose testament we had both written in good faith.

"Who are you, Walter? Be not a stranger, for I am in need of a friend."

"I am a worm and no man."

"A fitting answer, for truly it is worms you have become and thou art no longer a man."

I struggled to remember the rest of the Psalm: 'My God, My God, why hast thou forsaken me? Why art thou so far from helping me . . .?' I went no further. It was enough, for it did seem that I too would soon be a worm and no man and would directly have God's answer, but I did not want to think about that. Not yet.

"You never returned to Devon, Walter. Your mother died uncomforted in your love. Did you not know?"

"Aye."

"Aye, you did, or aye you did not?"

"Aye."

"Why did you leave her thus? She was old and alone."

"Home is a foreign place."

"True. I barely remember mine. My feeling is that home is a place of sorrow, no longer welcoming: my mother, father, sisters, all dead. I cannot recall their faces."

"My father beat me for no trespass. My mother starved me. My brothers tormented me. I could not abide it!"

"That is a lie, Walter, a lie that even Simon could not make convincing. Yet, admittedly, I too have often sinned against those who love me, then blame those who love me for my sins. It is a failing of all men, I trow."

"Exactly!"

"Not exactly, but more or less. Let us be truthful, for in this awful darkness truth is our only light." I smiled at my own bombast. "Lucy weeps for you, Walter. Do you not weep for her as well?"

"She was never mine."

"Ah! Smartly said. No one belongs to another, verily. Yet she did think you loved her."

"It was but a charity."

"But received in hope, Walter, a hope she nurtured. Oh, how a woman will nurture the frailest hope until it grows strong and multiplies. And when the loved one in her heart cannot abide, it is her own dead hopes for which she grieves. Yet from whence came our hopes if not from our beloved? Who then is responsible for our tears?"

"She was never mine."

"So you say." Poor Lucy. And Simon Ratiker, who speaks even now in my weary head, damn his miserable eyes!

Thus I remember my dialogue with a dead man, leading me into a twisted labyrinth of thought that frightened me. I retreated back to the dark silence of my prison where once again I sought sleep, but though lassitude lulled me into a stupor, I could not find it. If Simon should come, I would not be ready for him. Starving and parched, I would not have the strength to spar, and that would not do. I needed to restore some of my vigor for the game to come.

Finally I did sleep. I don't know when or how long. I awoke alert, though gagging on my tongue, and resolved to escape.

In sleep I had somehow devised a plan. The plan was there when I opened my eyes. It wanted only a spade for digging. Memory told me that to my right lay the clerk longest dead. With my back against the door, I took my bearings. Then, on hands and knees, I made my way over rotted lumps of flesh until I felt dry bones. He must have been a young man, this clerk. His bones were strong. I thanked God for this providence, begged the man for his forgiveness, and took his clavicle.

The earth beneath the door was stone solid so that I scraped more than dug with the bone. Occasionally I encountered a rock that worked free, leaving behind an area of crumbling dirt, but in general it was a slow effort. My former strength was a mere memory. Lack of food had taken its toll. Hours or what seemed hours of scraping and digging had produced no more than a depression the depth of a serving bowl — and only on my side of the door. I began to doubt I would ever again see the sun.

Not the sun, but light did come at long last: the light of a torch. Simon had returned.

This time he did not call to me, but stood silent on the other side of the door, listening.

Once again I waited in silence, and was rewarded by the sound of the bar being raised. The door swung open toward my crouching figure, concealing me from view. Simon entered, leading with his torch. He stepped into my pathetic escape hole, stumbled and fell, landing in the desiccated remains of Walter Bidick. He cried out as the torch fell from his hand.

We both grabbed for the torch at the same moment. It lay closer within my reach than his, but he was faster. His fingers closed around the handle of bound broom just as my fingers closed around his. Holding the torch between us, we rose together from the floor.

He chuckled in my face. "You are a surprising fellow, Clerk. I underestimated you by a long measure."

"My name is Jonathan Purchell," I said evenly.

"I know your name, but you are my clerk, are you not?" He wrested the torch from my grasp and backed away to block the open door. I now saw that his other hand held a cudgel.

"No," I replied. "I am no longer your clerk, nor your chronicler, nor your confessor, but on my own behalf I will happily discharge each of those employments. I wish to conclude this tale before I die."

He snorted. "No longer my clerk and never my confessor, yet will you be my intercessor? Methinks that is so. I charge you to speak for me at Heaven's Gate."

"Why would I do that?"

"Because in death you will have perfect understanding. You will know the truth of me and feel compassion. God will listen to you, Jonathan Purchell. You are clever with words. You have imagination."

"You surpass imagination, Rat Taker."

He chuckled again. "You cannot imagine interceding for my soul?"

"Nay, I cannot. Nor can any man lying here at your feet. They are as beyond caring for your soul as your soul is beyond redemption."

Using his cudgel, Simon scored a cross into the earthen wall. "Look upon this cross, Jonathan, then think of Him who hangs upon it while loving with a human heart all the humanity that does betray him. If you have ever suffered a single love betrayed, imagine then the depth and breadth of his suffering."

"Christ suffered, verily, but this is old news, is it not?"

"No, it is most timely, for He alone shares the solitary agony of every solitary soul and does embrace it for our redemption. He does, Jonathan. And He alone knows the sorrow I have borne these many years. Will he not show mercy?"

I backed away from this madding mangle of theology. It was too offensive. "Do not align your suffering with that of Our Lord's," I murmured. "It defiles all that is holy. And know you this, Rat Taker,

I will not offer up my death for your miserable soul. The Good Christ, as you say, has already provided you that service. Look to him alone for your salvation."

He gazed at me from the depths of his unfathomable eyes, his smile serene. "I will do that."

He lifted the torch higher. I feared he would set me afire before I could tell him my discovery.

"Simon," I said with a steadiness I did not feel. "Tell me, what happened here? I would hear the end of your tale before I die."

"There is no end," he whispered, his eyes sweeping around the walls. They wavered and stopped at the door leading to the underground passage. "There is no end."

"There is!" I prodded, driven beyond caution to break the boundaries of his memory. "Think you! What did you do after you saw them together?"

He shook his head while his lips moved to form words. I edged closer to hear. He threatened me with the torch, the madness bright in his eyes. I retreated to the far wall, not far from the underground passage.

"No escape through there," he warned.

"I know. But maybe answers hidden beneath the dust."

His eyes returned to the passage door and the madness within them dimmed.

"You barred the door," I ventured softly.

He returned his gaze sharply, alarmed. "What?"

"You barred the door and left them to die."

He rubbed his eyes with the back of his hand. "I blacked out. I don't remember. Perhaps I did . . . I don't remember."

"Before you blacked out, Simon, before that, you barred the door and left them. Then you made your way to the cellar stairs where you fainted. You were sick, so sick. Remember?"

He stared at me as if turned to stone.

"When you revived you heard the pounding . . ."

"In my head," he said quickly. "A pounding in my head. Pounding, pounding all the way up the stairs. I was blinded by the pain."

"Not in your head, Simon, from the passage behind the door. Amaury and Maude beating on the door, begging you to open the door. You could hear their cries!"

I waited for him to admit his crime. When he did not, I continued, "Perhaps you stumbled into the dark kitchen, found a weapon, returned to the cellar, and killed them. Is that how it went, Simon?"

"No!" he screamed. "No, I did not! Did I? No, I loved her too much. I would never kill her." He dropped the cudgel and began to sob. The torch suddenly seemed so heavy in his hand I expected it to fall as well. He lifted his tortured eyes to mine. "Did I? Did I kill her . . .?" I don't, I can't remember!

Pathetic man. So pathetic I could no longer muster a shred of pity for him. Leave him to God, I told myself. Wash your hands of him who would, in an instant, see you dead rather than see the truth of his trespasses. Truly, I felt him deserving of his damnation, yet I discovered my heart was not lacking in some compassion. I had come to know him too well. I knew his history, knew he was not always what he had become. I felt impelled to tell him my discovery.

"You did not kill her."

He stared at me stupidly, not daring to believe.

"You did not kill her," I repeated. "not Armury, not the dog. Think on it, Simon," I urged. "You were ill. You were drunk. You needed a lamp, but the simple act of returning to the house to get one confounded your purpose. That so, how could you have overcome the resistance of two strong people and a dog? It could never have happened that way, surely not."

"I barred the door," he said miserably. "And then I . . . I can't remember."

"Aye, you barred the door, and that was wrong. You knew it then, but you were too ill to consider how the wrong might be undone. You had strength only to crawl into your bed before delirium overtook you."

When I reached out to give him the silver cap, he flinched before accepting it. Confusion settled on his face as he rolled the object in his hand.

"Bidick found it. I suspect he may have divined the truth before he died. He was holding it in his grasp."

Simon glanced at the remains of Walter Bidick without a glimmer of remorse, and returned his gaze to the handle. "It is the handle of a walking stick," he murmured. He gazed up at me. "I've looked for it. Over and over did I look."

"I suspect Bidick found it buried in Maude's ashes."

His eyes went wide. "I never thought . . . !"

"How could you? You were not there. The question now is what meaning to make of it, Rat Taker. For myself, I believe it suggests a different truth about the death of the two lovers — a far different truth than you have all along feared."

A long silence stretched between us. I refrained from breaking it, allowing time for Simon to reach the same conclusion as I, and yet I feared he would not. A mere wink of hope could not bring truce to the tortured battle that had raged so long within him. I wondered if he were capable of ever finding peace. Simon was doomed to his hell regardless of what did or did not happen here years ago. He had murdered six men, since. How many more I would not venture to say, yet I amazed myself by wanting him to know the one crime he did not commit.

"It was he," he said with flat certainty. For a moment I believed the truth had broken through, but guilt and doubt were his element now. He could not draw a breath without them. "So think you?" he asked, his voice so small I could barely hear it.

"Aye, I do think," I replied wearily. "How else could it have been? Can you not see him? Think on it, Simon, your master entering the house after a night of drink and gaming. He is startled to hear pounding coming from below. He perhaps thinks it to be thieves. He lights a lamp and passes through the kitchen where he grabs his walking stick. Maude had been cleaning it. Remember? It is laying there on the sideboard ready to his grasp. Heavy it is, that walking stick, your master's weapon of choice when his anger is aroused. He carries it down into the cellar. And what does he find, Simon? What does he find?"

Simon had slipped down the doorframe so that he sat on the floor amid the scattered leaves of his testament. The torch tilted dangerously in his grasp, but he gave it no notice. His eyes were fixed on the passage door, perhaps seeing it closed with two living people on the other side.

"He finds them together," I say. "This large, strong man so possessive of his concubine, so quick to anger and to strike. He finds them together and is enraged."

Simon flung his arm across his eyes, as if to block his vision.

I edged toward my escape, distracting him with my own vision of that harrowing event so clear in my mind that I accepted it without reservation. "Maude holds the lamp. The master strikes her first, and the lamp sets her gown aflame as she falls to the ground. Amaury attacks in defense, but the heavy stick cracks his skull, maybe not with the first blow, nor the second, but eventually the bone breaks. And Pye, does she not try to defend the apprentice? Surely yes, but she too was killed or maimed during the fray. The walking stick, having done its work, drops into the flaming pyre that is Maude. All but the silver handle is consumed. The murderer retreats, thinking to clean up the remains on the morrow, but like so many others during those awful days, he goes healthily to bed, falls ill in his sleep, and never awakes."

Simon moaned and swayed while bracing the torch handle steady against the floor. Back and forth he swayed, his free hand clawing at the loose earth from my digging. Such excessive grief for such an old loss seemed unholy to me. But everything about this man was unholy. I could not condone his sins nor pity him his hell. In fact, I began to believe that it was only his fear of being guilty that had kept his love alive. To not love Maude, even after so many years, would have suggested more fully that he had killed her, and to that he could never confess. Now that the truth was revealed, I wondered if he would at last let go of that terrible love.

I wondered, aye, but I did not care. I picked up my journal and gingerly stepped around the distraught Simon and on through the door. "It is over," I said to him. "It is finished."

I don't know what I had expected. I had failed to look beyond the moment of my revelation, and, for the world, I was unprepared for Simon's last act. It began with a low chuckle that rose into a twittering giggle. My entire body urged me to flee to freedom, yet I remained on the threshold of that cursed room, unable to not watch the last remnants of Simon's sanity tear apart.

I could see everything within the chamber, wall-to-wall, door to door. Simon knelt to my left, near the wall where stood the stacks of manuscripts. Straight ahead was the door leading to the remains of Maude and Amaury, and beyond to where the passage walls stretched into darkness. Between the two doors lay six murdered men. Their bodies, made undulate by the flickering torch, seemed almost ready to heave upright and confront their murderer, but

even had that been possible there was no time. With swift and surprising deliberateness, Simon put the torch to the leaves of tender
parchment that had fallen from my hands. The floor was instantly
aflame. Rotted cloth and desiccated flesh shriveled to ash and fell
away from charred bones.

Simon rose to his feet and with, calm deliberateness, set afire
the stack of manuscripts. Of a sudden, I knew his final intention. I
almost cried, "No Simon!" but did not. I simply watched as he set
the torch to his hair. Then, himself a living torch, the man walked
through fire into the room opposite and laid himself over the remains of his Maude.

I could not have saved him. I made no move to try, but quickly
retreated from the searing heat and Simon's screams of agony
while uttering the only possible prayer: "God have mercy."

In veritate scribo,
Johannes P.

From the Journal of Jonathan Purchell
20 November, Anno Domini 1399
London, England

We pluck one perfect rose, we borrow another man's dog, we leave the master's gate ajar.

We are so thoughtless in our small acts, are we not? But more unaware than careless, I think. We simply cannot see how each act ties the shape of our lives to the lives of others until all the threads are linked.

And yet, I believe there are moments in which a man's destiny is cast. Sometimes a single act within an ordinary day does seal his fate. Good it is if, as a result, his life runs true to God's design, but who can say? There are those who argue that God's will is whatever is and no circumstance is outside of it. Others say, "Nay. That just as imperfect clay is shaped and fired into the perfect bowl, God accepts our lives wholly as we live them, all the while shaping them unto his Own Purpose." Who is to say one argument is so and the other is not? I do not say, but I know which argument I prefer.

Twenty-four years it has been since I wrote the conclusion to Simon's story. I now sit in my garden, old and very tired. My thoughts are frayed, my memories worn smooth, my soul reflective and poised for flight. My future belongs to eternity, a place I cannot surmise, nor do I wish to. I can only hope to be pleasantly surprised. Yet I sit here and ponder the mystery of God's Way within the ways of man, not because I am naturally given to deep thoughts, but because I once saw a burning man walk through fire and lay himself down in love. What is the meaning in something so far outside the ordinary? Why was I, of all men, given to be its witness? Now that I am nearing the full sum of my days, I do think on these things. How can I not?

My wife comes into the garden to serve me honeyed wine. My son Walter tucks a robe over my lap and under my feet. He adjusts another across my back. They pamper me, these two, and I let them. I call for my journal and a fresh quill. Walter knows what I require and quickly brings a small untidy book, dog-eared and faded with age. Then they leave, my wife and second son, while I return to that day long ago in which my destiny was sealed.

The fire did not destroy Simon Ratiker's house, being that the earthen chambers lay under the kitchen garden and not the house foundation. The rolling smoke retreated down the underground passage and the flames quickly began to subside. I closed the chamber door, doused it with buckets of water from the kitchen well, and let burn all that was beyond it. Somehow I had the presence of mind to also set aflame a pile of debris in the garden to account for the smell of smoke and to camouflage the smell of death. Such outdoor fires are prohibited within the city, of course, and violators are fined, but the ruse was well worth a few shillings.

I closed the house that very day, leaving a note to Widow Truwet saying that Simon had sailed to the Continent on business and was not exact on his date of return. Then I moved to an inn outside the city walls where I stayed for a fortnight. I could not tolerate so soon the company of the ghosts in that tragic house. I calculated the length of my imprisonment in Simon's cellar: two nights and three days. Too long, too long, yet even now, I return often to that place or one much like it in the twisted truths of dream.

The year of that day in 1375 in which Simon's life ended, brought another visitation of plague. The pestilence arrived in the city of London three weeks after Simon died, stayed through the winter and into the spring. As in former visitations, though the mortality was not so high, the pestilence provided an easy excuse for excess, greed and vice. Many a man profited through another man's demise and rejoiced for it.

For myself, I freely admit that I in no way intended to reveal what had happened in the cellar, for I feared the reasonable suspicions of the Court should it investigate. Only by utmost circumspect did I cheat the odds of discovery.

My story was that Simon returned from abroad and died at home from an unknown cause. The ashes raked from the cellar and shoveled into hemp bags filled a single coffin. No one asked to examine the remains; they were only too glad that the box was nailed shut. I then submitted Simon's accounts to the Court of the Exchequer. Most dutifully did I submit them without offering explanations. Should they discover minor alterations in Simon's signature from the time I began to manage the books, I knew they would also discover that the accounts were accurate. I then left the house to the Warden's keeping and, after a few weeks, found another employment. I lived modestly for almost a year, being for all to see an honest clerk.

It took nearly a month of search and inquiry, I was told, for the Court deputy to find me, and he would have failed in his attempt had I not returned each week for a meal at Widow Truwet's tavern. The widow put me wise, as I had expected she would, to the deputy's inquiries. Within that week, possibly on the very day, I reported to the Court where I was informed that a will found among

Simon's papers documented how he wished to apportion his estate. Except for the customary charities to assure his entry into heaven, he had left all to me. The deputy handed me the document written and signed in the jagged script I knew so well. To disguise any hint of my foreknowledge, I collapsed senseless on the floor. The most suspicious man alive would not have doubted my surprise.

Thus did the House of Ratiker become the House of Purchell, and the usual business of living did follow. My fears that the past would cloud any future within that house were soon set to rest. The future brought forth its own measure of vicissitudes. The past lay buried. Simon's ghost had no quarrel with me.

Today I am enjoying my garden, a quiet sanctuary within the city. Here is where my children played. I see them still, always young, running between the lemon trees. Clover grass carpets the lime pit. Purple gillyflowers or blue gentian, depending on the season, borders the walks. My wife grows herbs of every hue of green in the kitchen garden where I once burned debris. All is smoothed over, made clean. The cellar doors are locked. No one ventures into that place where only memories remain, and in memory do I go there now.

I am standing once again outside that fiery chamber, staring at the burning man. I ask myself, who is this rat taker, this 'no man' who resembles all men in their secret guilt and sorrow?

Simon Ratiker was a murderer, and this I cannot condone. Nor do I pity him his damnation. Yet I am bound to consider how events conspired against him. To consider also how, most coldly, I allowed him to go to his death without the benefit of the Last Rites. I did, verily. I could have stayed his last act. I could have dragged him from the flames, yet I did not. Even the Hand of God, it seems, obscured evidence that might have saved his sanity if not his very soul?

I think on this and am confounded, yet, as much as I might wish it, I cannot unravel the threads of another man's fate. I can only call to my abiding belief that He who can do all things will most surely do the one thing that fulfills His Purpose: to bring those He created out of His Love back into His Love.

To this purpose, no suffering is wasted. So said Father Liam those many years ago. From the deepest cry to the smallest tear nothing is wasted within the symmetry of redemption. And if this be true, would such an economy not also include the souls suffering in Hell? For then, on that day when all souls are called unto Heaven, they too will come forth from a Hell that is no more, thus fulfilling God's purpose most completely.

The year is 1399. This calamitous century draws to a close. War and rebellion, famine and pestilence, all manner of strife did mark its many days. I pray humankind will never see another like it. As well these events did mark my days, for I am a man of this time and of this world. Now, as I sit within my garden, I can feel the world receding as my time of Judgment draws nearer — and I tremble. My life has not been blameless. Yet I do trust that the Lord, whatever His will, will not forsake me. Nor that Simon Ratiker, the man whom I have come to love in faith, does ever abide in me: Simon Ratiker, that wretched No Man who is All Men, ever burning in the cellar of my soul where, to this day, the rats of London thrive.

In veritate scribo,
Johannes P.

Visit us at *www.qpbooks.com*.

www.ingramcontent.com/pod-product-compliance
Lightning Source LLC
Chambersburg PA
CBHW051346020726
47501CB00007B/2296